Family Sh

By John Nixon

Chapter One

It was a hot and sultry afternoon, during those 'dog days' of late summer; a time that the ancients believed was influenced by the rising of Sirius, the Dog Star. The sun was hot and the air still; nothing moved without effort, and any effort was only rewarded with more heat. In a few days time the schools would open their doors again, the teachers would return from their holidays in the Camargue or Tuscany, and the children would reinhabit their special world. So would begin their noisy, downhill dash towards Christmas, with its bright lights and brash commercialism.

But today there was no noise. It was as if the heat had sucked out any semblance of activity from young and old alike. An occasional car drove by, windows open, its occupants seeking in vain for some respite from the oppression.

The garden at 22 Edward Street was long and thin. The house had been built just before the First World War, and was of red brick. It was one of a row of houses in the older part of the town, built originally for tradesmen and shopkeepers, and which now had that air of solidity so sought after. The garden had been cared for over many years by its previous owner, but the current owner was less keen, although she did try to keep the lawn cut and the weeds at bay.

The trees and shrubs which lined the garden were past their best. The leaves drooped in the heat, as if preparing to fall, and what flowers there were, were overblown and tired, with browning edges, burnt by the sun. The grass on the lawn was dry and brown, the only green being the weeds which forced their way into places where they were not welcome.

The sun had made the garden too hot to be in. The patio bricks scorched underfoot, and the chairs kept in the garden for sunny days were too hot to sit on. The kitchen, which was at the back of the house and overlooked the patio and garden, afforded some shelter from the heat.

From the window the entire garden could be seen, apart from the very end which dipped away from the house towards the river. With the back door and windows open they were able to enjoy lunch in the shade, but have the benefit of the garden view.

It was after that lunch. She was standing in the kitchen, with her back to the door which led into the rest of the house. She was quite tall and slim, with fair hair cropped short. In deference to the weather she was wearing a cooling blouse and light summer skirt. She did not hear him coming up behind her until he put his hands gently on her waist. He slid his hands upwards inside her blouse. She leaned backwards into him.

'Mmm, that's nice,' she said, 'but it's so hot.'

She pushed his hands away and he moved them downwards, over her skirt. She turned and smiled at him over her shoulder as he rested his hands on her abdomen, imagining the life growing there, which she had just told him about that day. As he did so he gazed out of the window down the garden, picturing his wife, comparing her in his mind's eye.

'You are pleased, aren't you?' she asked. She had asked him earlier when she had told him the news, but wanted reassurance.

'You know that I am. I think it's wonderful that you're going to have our baby.'

'But there are going to have to be changes somehow, aren't there?'

He maintained his gaze and continued his imaginings of his wife, and he started to consider the options open to him.

'Yes, of course,' he replied, almost absent-mindedly.

She turned right round to him and kissed him, which he returned as his mind raced.

The police officers stood on the doorstep, knocking loudly on the door and calling out. There was no answer.

'Break it down.'

A burly uniformed officer swung the 'enforcer' against the front door, which splintered as the lock broke and the door swung open. Running into the premises they heard screams from the kitchen, and as they went into the room they saw a knife smeared with blood, which had been dropped on to the floor, and heard the choking gasps of a stab victim. One of the police officers rushed to apply pressure to the wound as he called for an ambulance, but it seemed as if it may well be too late as the blood spurted across the floor. The remaining officers escorted the other person in the room, now silent and in shock, out to the waiting police car.

The police station in Hopley was an unattractive 1960s-built concrete block. There were two steps up from the pavement to a pair of glass doors which gave into a lobby that was spartan in the extreme. Posters warning of various potential crimes and how to keep you safe at night adorned the peeling walls. The vinyl-covered floor was clean but unwelcoming. A glass partition kept the public away from the police officers who manned the station. A door at the far end of the lobby, protected with a code lock, led through to the interview rooms and inner offices.

The interview room being used was similar to the lobby. A metal-framed table with a scarred veneer top, together with four tubular-legged chairs were the only pieces of furniture, apart from the sound recording equipment. A grubby window looked out on to a backyard, around which crisp packets and plastic carrier bags blew, together with other rubbish which had been carried there on the wind from the nearby marketplace.

There were two police officers in the room. Detective Inspector Henry Brookes [Harry] was in his early thirties, just over six feet tall, slim and smart, with an eye for fashion. His colleague Detective Constable James Cook was of a similar age and height, but rounder and rather more untidy in his appearance. They both had plenty of experience in dealing with serious crime, and so it was natural they had been assigned to this case. This was to be their first interview with the suspect, and they wanted to get an overview of the case before addressing the details. Harry always liked to try to understand the suspect and his or her motivation which led on to the commission of a serious crime. Once he had done that, he felt more able to comprehend the many bits and pieces of evidence that he would need to be able to bring a suspect to justice.

Having been brought into the station two hours previously after being arrested at the scene, the suspect had been in the cells since then, but was now sitting at the interview room table, alongside the advising solicitor. Harry Brookes made the introductions for the two officers for the PACE recordings, and the suspect and solicitor introduced themselves. Harry spoke first.

'So what's been going on?' he said encouragingly.

James Cook smiled to himself as he had seen Harry do this before, not brow-beating but gently leading his suspect to reveal all.

'What's happened? Why did you do it?'

The solicitor leaned towards his client and whispered some advice. His client nodded.

'The full story,' Harry said, again encouragingly.

The suspect settled into the chair and began to speak.

'It'll never all fit in.'

Michael Downing stood in the living room of the flat he shared with his wife Fiona and his twin daughters, Grace and Victoria, who was known to everyone, except her father, as Vicky. The twins were heading off to Birmingham University for their first term. The anxiety surrounding the exams back in the summer, and the tense wait for the results now seemed to be all worthwhile. The excitement had been building for the girls for over a month now. No one in their family had ever been to university, so it was something of an adventure. Indeed, when Michael was at school, he and his parents had lived in a council house, and money had always been tight. Whether able or not, university was something that could only be aspired to by someone from his background. Since receiving confirmation of their places, both girls had been making lists of things to take; clothes,, laptops, iPods, as well as the more mundane items of household equipment they would need in their new life away from home. Shopping trips had been planned and executed, so-called essentials as well as actual essentials bought, and the resultant packages, along with what seemed to be a mountain of foodstuffs, were piled high in the room.

Grace and Victoria were eighteen and a half years old; their mother, Michael's previous wife, Louise, had been killed in a car crash. The twins shared the same outlook on many things. They liked the same clothes, the same music, the same films and sometimes even the same boys, although that had not been a major problem. Unusually for twins they were not especially alike in looks. Victoria was slightly taller and fairer than Grace, and wore spectacles, which gave her a somewhat 'academic' look, which she turned to her advantage. Grace and Victoria had both had a variety of boyfriends whilst at school, but nothing serious enough to get in the way of their exciting future plans. On the university open days they had attracted attention from other potential students, so they were looking forward to starting their new life.

Michael and Fiona had been married for fourteen years but had no children of their own. It was not their choice, indeed Fiona would have liked to have had children, but it simply had not happened that way. He was rapidly approaching his sixtieth birthday and had been running the Hopley Bookshop for eighteen years. He was just over six feet tall, with now-thinning sandy-coloured hair. He liked to keep fit and in his younger days had been a member of the local athletics club where he had lived. He enjoyed dressing smartly, and would usually be seen in a crisp casual shirt and jacket whilst at work. Not for him the scruffy dress-down appearance so beloved of employers and employees alike these days. His car was equally clean and smart. When he took over the bookshop in his early forties he had felt his best running days were behind him, but he had joined the local tennis club, and had been a regular player ever since. During that time he had served as a committee member, treasurer and club captain at varying times.

Fiona was forty-one years old, and before her marriage to Michael she had worked in the claims department of Unity Insurance in the town. She was slim with shoulder-length chestnut brown hair. She had turned heads when she was younger, and even now, in her early forties, she was frequently the recipient of admiring glances. As the girls had grown up she had returned to work part-time and now worked two days a week at Unity, as well as helping in the bookshop at busy times. Her parents, David and Megan Lewis, worked and lived in the town. David was a sales executive at the Toyota dealership, and Megan worked on the checkout at Tesco's.

It was through David Lewis that Michael had bought his car, a Toyota Avensis, which was now parked at the back of the shop, outside the door to the flat, waiting to be loaded.

'It won't all fit in. You'll have to thin it down somehow,' Michael repeated.

'Oh, Dad!' Grace and Victoria chorused. 'You always say that.'

It was true. He did always say that. Not that

they had been away to university before, but whenever they had been going on holiday, going to see friends, or that time when they went on a French exchange trip to Rouen. On that occasion they had tried to take everything they owned so that they did not feel too homesick. It was always the same, but he always tried to fit in everything they wanted and, so far, had always been successful. But looking at the mountain of items Michael was unsure that he could pull it off this time.

As he started to reduce the pile in the flat, and slowly but surely fitted the various items into nooks and crannies in the car, Michael's mind went back to the girls when they were tiny, and newborn. Helpless but smiley is how he remembered them. Then their first day at school, pretty as a picture in their pressed skirts and blouses, complete with excited faces. Their first dates, and the hours spent in the bathroom preparing. And tears as their hearts were broken by the same date. Now was their first venture into the world on their own, without him, or Fiona, or Louise. It was always 'their' not 'her' as they seemed to do most things together, even joint dates. He had difficulty imagining them being apart, but that would come soon enough, they were after all going to be studying different subjects, Grace, International History and Politics, and Victoria, Medieval English, so they probably would not have too much time together.

Michael stopped packing the car as he drifted off into this reverie, but he was brought back to reality by a voice from the kitchen.

'I've done you some lunch to take with you,' Fiona was calling.

'Thanks Mum,' two voices replied in unison.

Michael returned to his loading duties. Most of the mountain had now disappeared and he was not quite sure where it had gone, he only knew that with the twins in the car as well, being able to see out was going to prove difficult. When he had finally slotted the last piece of the jigsaw together, he went back into the kitchen where the girls were picking up the packed lunch that Fiona had prepared for them. Michael took his wallet out of his pocket and, opening it, took out ten ten pound notes. He gave five notes to each twin.

'Just to get you started, in case you have forgotten something. Although I can't see what,' he added, looking out towards the heavily laden Toyota, and then looking back towards Grace and Victoria, smiling.

'Thanks Dad,' again both girls spoke together as they gave him a hug.

'Now, are you sure you've got all your paperwork? Student Loan form? Registration documents? Course details and reading lists? Any other identification documents or anything?'

'Yes Dad, don't panic and fuss. We've got everything we need,' came the reply.

'Right, let's go.'

Michael said goodbye to Fiona, and the twins hugged and kissed her.

'See you at Christmas, or before maybe'

Fiona watched them drive away, and like Michael had been, she was transported back so many years to when they were young. She remembered babysitting for Michael and Louise when the twins were babies and toddlers, and she remembered Michael, after Louise died, struggling to cope with two little girls. As a regular customer in the bookshop she had met Louise on a number of occasions as well as knowing Michael. He was always friendly and very charming; she thought it was partly why the bookshop was so successful. He had an effortless manner which endeared him to customers of all ages, both men and women.

She had become close to Michael in the weeks and months after Louise's death, which was at the beginning of October 1996, fifteen years ago almost to the day, and they had married at the end of July the following year. The girls had always been fond of Fiona, so that had not been a problem, and when Michael and Fiona had no children of their own she adopted them as her daughters. So seeing them drive off with Michael was a wrench for Fiona as well as for Michael, but she was confident that they would do well and enjoy themselves, and she looked forward to seeing them at Christmas, and hopefully before then.

It was a two-hour drive from Hopley to Birmingham University, taking into account the city centre driving after leaving the main roads. Michael had driven it before when he had brought the twins on their interview day. What did we do before satnav he wondered? As usual for first-year students, Grace and Victoria were accommodated in Halls of Residence, and Michael found the block which was to be their home for the next year. Parking nearby was a little tricky but he finally managed it, and then began the laborious task of emptying the car of its contents and carrying it all across to the flats. Grace and Victoria helped; it was easier unloading than loading, and soon they were settled and meeting other freshers. Michael felt a little in the way, so after a quick cup of tea he left them to it. As he kissed them goodbye and walked back towards the now empty car he felt a sudden surge of loneliness, and remembered when he had last felt like this. Then he thought about Fiona at home awaiting his return, and he remembered how much happiness she had brought back into his life so many years ago.

The late summer sun was beating down as he drove home, and rather than put the air conditioning on in the car he opened the windows, enjoying the breeze.

Paula Hamilton settled herself into a chair in the corner of Fiona Downing's kitchen. Paula's comfortable frame was a perfect match for the chair, which even Michael referred to as 'Paula's chair'. The smell of fresh coffee filled the kitchen, and although Fiona herself was a tea drinker only, she kept the coffee for her regular morning chats with her long-time friend, who lived close by. Two of Paula's three children were already at university and the eldest was in the Army, serving overseas, so she understood how Fiona was feeling about the 'loss' of her girls.

'Have you heard from them yet, then? We didn't hear from either of ours for over a week. They were too busy enjoying themselves to think about phoning home.'

'It was only yesterday they went, it's a bit early,' Fiona replied, although wishing in her heart that either or both of the twins had phoned yesterday evening, after Michael had left them, and they had moved in.

'You know that if you ever want to go to see

them during the week I can always do an extra day in the shop.'

Paula worked in the bookshop on Mondays, giving Michael and Fiona a two day weekend, and she was very willing to do extra days. She felt quite lonely now that her family were away for most of the year, and she welcomed the company and friendship of the regular customers, whom she had got to know well over the years she had been there.

'The main reason for them ringing home is usually culinary or medical. Either they want advice on how to cook something, or to ask advice on some food that's gone off, or they've acquired some bug or other, and need information on how to deal with it.'

Fiona let Paula's chatter flow over her as she continued to think about Grace and Victoria in their new surroundings. She would have liked to have gone with them yesterday, but it had not been practical with everything they had to take with them. She cast her mind back to Louise and wondered, rather sadly, what she would think of her girls, so grown up now. As she did so she welled up inside and a small tear formed at the corner of her eye.

Paula stopped her chatter, noticing that her friend was upset.

'I'm sorry, Fi, I shouldn't run on. Why didn't you tell me to shut up? I know I can go on too much. Is it the girls? '

'No, not really,' Fiona replied. She hesitated. 'Well, it is in a way.'

'Come on; tell all, what's the matter?'

'It's Louise. I was thinking about her and how proud she would have been about her girls.'

'They're just as much yours, you brought them up. You can take as much if not more credit for how they have turned out.'

'Yes, I suppose so. But I was just picturing them when I saw them for the first time after their mother had died in that terrible crash. Three years old, not really understanding, but just standing there saying "Mummy's gone to heaven" with tears streaming down their little cheeks. Even after Michael and I got married it was some time before they started calling me Mum.   But now I don't think they can even remember Louise and I think that's a shame.'

'Fiona.'

Michael was calling from the shop.

Fiona dabbed at her eyes.

'I'd better go.   It can get busy on Tuesdays because of the publishers' reps Michael sees.'

'I'll come with you if you like,' said Paula.

'Yes, thanks.'

Both women walked out of the kitchen, through a small inner hall and through another door which led in to the stockroom at the back of the shop. As they walked into the main area of the shop, they saw the rep waiting to one side while Michael continued to serve an elderly lady, a regular of many years standing. His easy manner and charm were there for all to see, and just for a moment Fiona wondered, ever so briefly, if that was what had attracted her to the shop in the first place, when she was just a new customer, and whether she had already been a little in love with him before Louise had died. She put these thoughts away almost before she had thought them, but thought them she had.

Michael looked up,

'Hello Paula, come to check up on us now we are "empty-nesters"?'

'I don't think you are just yet, Michael,' she replied. Paula was one of the few women, it seemed, who was impervious to Michael's charm. Her marriage to Peter, who was ten years older than her, had been long and very happy. Their three children were well-adjusted, and life was good for them. Having known Fiona since school she didn't let Michael come between them, and he recognised this.

'Can you hold the fort, Fiona, while I see what goodies the publishers have on offer this month? I'll be about an hour.'

'Yes, off you go.'

Michael disappeared into the stockroom with the rep, leaving Fiona and Paula together in the shop.

'Are you okay now, Fi?'

Nobody else called Fiona Fi, and nobody ever had done, apart from Paula, and that started when they were at school when everyone had nicknames or shortened names of some sort. And it had just stuck.

'Yes, I am, but I'm still thinking about Louise. Maybe I should do something for the girls to remind them of their mother; a folder or something, with photos and details.'

'Yes,' Paula said slowly. 'You would have to be careful not to reopen old wounds. But what about Michael? What would he think? It could be worse for him.'

'I don't think I would tell him at first. Just see how it worked out, what I could put together.'

'Then I would ask him what he thinks before giving whatever I have done to the girls.'

Customers came and went in the shop. Fiona enjoyed it when it was busy. She liked chatting to the customers, finding the books they were looking for, and recommending new authors to those customers whose favourite authors were not writing as quickly as they could read them.

As lunchtime approached Paula said she would have to go as she had other shopping to be done, but she suggested that she and Fiona got together that evening as she had an idea that might help. Fiona said that Michael was playing tennis and so she would come round about seven.

'See you later, then, and I'll tell you my idea.'

Fiona, intrigued, said goodbye and spent the rest of the day at home, wondering what this idea was.

'What is it then? This big idea?'

Fiona had been wondering all afternoon what Paula was going to come up with. Michael had left for his game of tennis quite early, the evenings were getting shorter now, and so Fiona had been able to arrive at Paula's promptly.

'Trace their family tree. If you want to give Grace and Vicky something that you think will help them link into the family, trace their family tree and intersperse it with photos of the ancestors from different generations.'

Fiona looked uncertain.

'Do you really think they would be interested? Surely they are more concerned about the future, not the past?'

She thought again.

'I suppose it might work if I can find photos of them and their Mum, and put them together with pictures of Michael's family. I don't know very much about Louise's family though,' she said.

Fiona had seen various television programmes on the subject of tracing one's family tree, but suspected that it was not quite as straightforward as portrayed.

'What would I need to start?'

'Names and photos, if possible, of as old a relative or relatives as you know,' Paula replied 'Granny, granddad or even great-grands if possible. Who do you know?'

'Well, I know that Michael's parents were James and Anne Downing, I know he was a postman, and I don't think she ever went out to work, but they died a long time ago. About the time the twins were born, I think. I don't know any further back than that. I can't ask him, anyway, because I don't want him to know I am doing this for the girls, at least, not yet. Maybe I could start with my own family, just to get in practice. My Mum and Dad are still around and they might be able to help.'

'Good idea. I got a book out of the library this afternoon and it gives you an outline of how to start,' Paula said. 'There are variety of websites that can point you in the right direction, and some which list census details and births, marriages and deaths.'

'If I'm going to look at my own family first, that should be quite easy. My Mum's maiden name was Megan Evans and I know the name of my grandmother, my Mum's mother. She was Hannah Cartwright, before she married Evan Evans. Very Welsh! I also know that she was born on New Year's Day 1915, but I am not sure where. If I get a copy of her birth certificate that will tell me her parents names, and also her mother's maiden name, as well as where she was born. We'll be off then.'

Fiona was suddenly all excited. She liked the idea of constructing a family tree not only for Grace and Victoria, but also for herself. This was the first step. Fiona and Paula ordered the birth certificate for Hannah online, and a week later it duly arrived. Fiona was not expecting anything exceptional, but she was intrigued by one piece of information on it. As well as giving the place and date of birth, the time was given also, 3.10pm. She knew her own birth certificate did not have her time of birth on, and neither did any others she had ever seen. As she thought, this was not going to be as easy as those on television. Perhaps the book that Paula had borrowed from the library would be able to explain. She rang Paula to see if she still had the book, which fortunately she did. Fiona suggested that she should come over.

Chapter Five

Michael Downing was feeling quite happy with life. After the upheavals of years gone by, financial scrimping, losing his job at the library in Emberton, the worry surrounding taking on the new business and then with his wife being killed, his life was more measured now. He missed his daughters, of course, but knew that they would be back soon and they would speak on the telephone from time to time. The bookshop was trading steadily, and Fiona seemed very happy. What was there to disturb him? Nothing it would seem.

Before Louise's accident Fiona had been a regular customer, calling in during her lunch-hour. Michael had loved Louise very much, but he had become very friendly with Fiona, and had been pleased when she had offered to babysit the twins for them. It was as if he had almost unacknowledged feelings for her. When Louise died he was comforted by his work in the shop and meeting his regular customers, one of whom was Fiona. She continued to help out with the twins in the early months after Louise's death and gradually she and Michael became closer and closer. Louise had died in October 1996, and by the spring of 1997 Michael and Fiona had become very fond of each other and they decided to marry, which they did at the end of July.

Now they were on their own for the first time ever. Although it was fifteen years since she had died, Louise still loomed large in Michael's mind. However he did not mention this to Fiona or anyone else. Spending more time on his own, with the girls away and Fiona working at Unity Insurance two days a week, Michael thought more and more about what had happened in the run up to the accident. He went to the cemetery to visit her grave and place flowers there regularly, but he kept these visits secret from Fiona, and was careful no one saw him. He did not have any very close friends, and although he played tennis at the local club, usually with Derek Smithers, a local solicitor, he had no one with whom he could share such confidences. He did have a brother, Ian, who was three years younger than him, but they had not spoken for the best part of twenty years. They did not even send Christmas cards to each other. The reasons for this lay buried in the distant past, and he did not wish to disturb the past.

His life was the bookshop, and as long as he could keep that going he would be content. He looked forward to seeing the new titles that were being published month by month, trying to spot the trends so he could stay up-to-date with his stock. His previous experience as a library assistant also gave him a wide knowledge of public tastes, and he had built on this during his years at Hopley Bookshop. His formal education may have been fairly ordinary, he had left school at sixteen with just five 'O' levels, but he had worked hard to acquire a formidable general knowledge, which assisted immensely when dealing with customer enquiries. Fiona was happy and very supportive, the twins were settled and there seemed no reason why life would not continue along the same lines in the future. He had so much to lose if it did not.

He did not recognise Sam Wainwright when he walked into the shop, but then neither did Sam realise who Michael was.

'Do you sell Ordnance Survey Maps?' Sam asked.

'Yes, over here.' Michael pointed to a shelf full of Landranger and Explorer maps.

'I'm new to the area, so I need to find my way around.'

Michael's natural customer friendliness swung into action; it was only later he wished it hadn't.

'Have you moved in locally, then?' Michael enquired.

'No. I've just got a new area to cover. I'm a rep for Harpers Seeds and I'm visiting Hopley Garden Centre initially, but I need to know the area. I always think that these Landrangers are ideal for that. I live down in Emberton so it is a pretty big area to cover. I didn't have a map which stretched this far.'

'I used to live in Emberton.'

Michael stopped and realised what he had said. It was too late now to undo it, but he wished he had kept his mouth shut.

Sam looked at him again, puzzled. Then it was as if a light had been switched on.

'You're Michael Downing aren't you?'

'Ye-e-s.' Michael hesitated, trying to work out the connection.

'Emberton Runners?' Sam reminded him.

Michael thought he was talking about bean seeds, but then he remembered.

'Sam Wainwright?   Now I remember.   You were the skinny 800 metres hope. What happened?'

Sam looked down at his too round stomach.

'Too much beer, too many pies, not enough training I'm afraid.   Are you still involved with training young hopefuls?'

'No. I gave that up when we moved here. I do play a bit of tennis, though, just to keep in trim.'

Sam looked enviously at Michael's slim figure.

'Look, I'm in Hopley overnight. I'm staying at the WaggonandHorses down the road. Why don't you come and have a drink with me tonight, just to chew over old times?'

Michael realised he could not say no, but he did not really want to say yes. Emberton was better left in the past, he thought. He was worried that Sam might bring it all too clearly into the present.

'What are you having Mike? Pint?'

Sam Wainwright's voice squeaked across the bar of the WaggonandHorses.

Michael Downing disliked 'Mike' in the same way that he disliked 'Fi' and 'Vicky', but with some people it was unavoidable.

'Thanks, Sam. Bitter, yes.'

He didn't really know why he didn't dislike 'Sam' as opposed to Samuel for the same reason. Maybe it was because that was how he had known him from the outset.

The WaggonandHorses was the main pub in the high street in Hopley. It was one of the oldest buildings in the town and had once been a coaching inn. The bar was comfortable and welcoming, with an interesting menu for bar snacks which reflected the owners' Mediterranean origins. There were four bed and breakfast rooms, one of which was currently occupied by Sam Wainwright. Michael was not a pub-goer generally so he was unable to hazard an opinion on the beers that were stocked, but he did know that it always seemed busy, both lunchtimes and evenings, so he assumed that the drinks were as good as the food.

He sat down at one side of the bar, having been brought his drink by a young barman who smiled at him and made him feel uncomfortable all at the same time. He had not been keen to come for this drink, as he was unsure what Sam might say. It was many years since he had lived in Emberton, and it seemed a lifetime away. He decided to play safe.

'Why did you give up the running?'

'I suppose the truth of it was I wasn't as good as I thought I was. I used to enjoy the training that we did together, and that continued after you left. I liked being fit, and I liked the races. Trouble was that as time went by I stopped getting any better, and there were youngsters coming along who started beating me.'

Michael thought it was a familiar tale. A bright young prospect suddenly realising he was not going to be the next gold medal winner. It was always difficult when that stage came along. Should you carry on for the love of it, or is it too difficult to face the truth, and better to leave them to it? Michael had never been that good, although he had enjoyed the competition, so it was easier for him to take a step backwards.

'Is that when you stopped?' he asked

'No. I carried on for a while, and I helped with the training as well, rather like you did. But then I got bored by it all and found other interests. When I was running seriously I had little time for girls, but then once I stopped winning races, I realised what I'd been missing out on. All my energy started being used elsewhere instead of running.'

He said this with something of a leer, which Michael found rather distasteful.

'What about you, Mike? How's your wife?

Michael hesitated momentarily before answering.

'Sadly she was killed in a car crash fifteen years ago, and I have remarried since then. What about you? How long have you been in the seed business? Did you marry one of those girls who tempted you away from the track?'

'Yes, I did. Didn't work out, though. Divorced two years ago; no kids thankfully. That's when I got this job travelling around. Gets me out of town. Sorry to hear about your wife. I remember seeing her once or twice at functions at the Runners. Debby, Deborah wasn't it?'

'No, no. My wife's name was Louise.'

'Oh, sorry. Must be muddling her up with someone else. Dark hair, curvy?'

'Not my wife, Sam. That must be somebody else's. It's all those girls, you're getting confused.'

'It's all the beer over the years, fuddled the memory.' He grinned as he made his way over to the bar and refilled his glass and Michael's.

'Nice little town, Hopley. The garden centre is busy so it looks as if I shall be returning soon. How's the book trade?'

Michael felt on slightly safer ground.

'Fine. We've been here a long time now and are well established. I think that counts for a lot in a small town. Must be the same with the Garden Centre?'

Sam returned to his thoughts about Emberton.

'You worked in the library, didn't you? You recommended books on athletics training to me which I couldn't afford to buy, and I used to come and borrow them. Attractive looking bird there, I remember. Tall, fair, very nice.'

Michael bristled.

'That was my wife.'

Unusually Sam had the decency to blush.

'Sorry, Mike. Didn't mean anything. Er, look, I think I'd better go now, got an early start tomorrow.'

Embarrassed, he drank the rest of his pint and walked swiftly away.

'See you next time I visit,' he called back.

'Don't rush back,' Michael mumbled.

He finished his drink and left the pub. As he walked back along the high street he thought about what Sam had said. Still, he wouldn't be returning for some time yet. When he arrived home Fiona was curled up watching television. He had told her that he was going out for a drink with the seed rep from Emberton.

'Had a nice time?' she asked.

'OK. Not a lot in common, really. I think he thought I was somebody else from Emberton.'

Michael was feeling on edge and did not want to have a long chat with Fiona about Sam so he finished the conversation there. Fiona had always found Michael to be very open about the past, so it was odd that he should be defensive. What was it about Sam that so disconcerted him?

Chapter Six

Fiona was a fair-weather gardener. The garden which belonged to the flat was long and thin, and well-established over the years since the flats ands shops had been built. It was also slightly unusual, as it was across the road which ran along behind the shop. All the shops in the row in which the bookshop was situated had flats above them, most of them occupied by the shop owners. The road at the back enabled deliveries to be made, provided parking spaces for the occupants of the flats, and also gave a more private entrance to the living accommodation than was possible from the front. Fiona had worked hard in the garden during the fourteen years she had been living over the shop, and she enjoyed the privacy and colour it afforded. That said, on a chilly Saturday afternoon in October, she was not encouraged to do those autumnal garden tasks which she knew had to be done. Pruning, cutting and clearing deadwood were jobs for another day, she decided. Michael also liked the garden, but more from the point of view of receiving the benefits it gave, rather than getting his hands dirty to create the benefits in the first place.

From the kitchen window she could look across the road and through the white wicket gate which led through to the garden. Had she had boys not girls no doubt the lawn would have been Wembley Stadium, Lords or Wimbledon, depending on the time of year. With the girls there was less pressure on the garden, but they had still enjoyed playing their games there, riding their bikes around the paths and in between the trees at the far end, and Wimbledon would still make an occasional appearance. From her viewpoint she could just see the last of the roses, the red penstemon and the bright, sunny yellow of the rudbeckia brightening up the garden before winter closed over it.

'Rather late for the rudbeckia,' she thought.

Although it was a flat and not a house Fiona felt very settled and happy here, although she thought sometimes that her parents, who lived in a large, modern house on the edge of town, would have preferred her and Michael to have bought a place of their own away from the town centre.

Since Paula had first suggested it, Fiona had become really keen on the idea of creating a family tree. She surfed the Internet and found and subscribed to a couple of websites which gave access to census records and births, marriages and deaths records. While she was waiting for her grandmother's birth certificate to arrive she had been exploring other relatives of hers. She was anxious to involve Michael and his family as soon as possible, but she wanted to make some progress with the folder for the twins first. She was, therefore, looking forward to Paula's visit to tell her what she had found, and to look further into the apparent oddity she had found on Hannah Cartwright's birth certificate.

'Hello, Fi.'

Fiona jumped. She had been drifting off in a daydream, staring out of the window, when Paula knocked on the kitchen door and opened it.

'Sorry, did I startle you? You were off with the

fairies.'

Fiona regained her composure.

'Hello, Paula, sorry, do come in.'

Paula had already come in and was settling herself in her chair.

'I'll put the kettle on,' Fiona said, ' Tea okay for you as it's afternoon?'

'Yes, thanks. Have you heard from those girls yet?'

'Yes, Thursday. They're in the middle of fresher's week at the moment, so it seems to be all play and no work until Monday, when it all starts in earnest.'

Fiona busied herself getting cups and saucers out of the cupboard; she really didn't like tea in mugs.

'I was looking at the garden and remembering how the girls played there when they were little. Oh dear, their going away keeps bringing back memories. I think I have done nothing else this week since they went but wallow in nostalgia. It probably wasn't as good and rosy as I am remembering.'

'It never is,' Paula replied. 'But it helps us only to remember the good bits. We would be very miserable if all we remembered was when they had runny noses from a cold, tears from being teased at school, or arguments over who had been in the bathroom too long.'

Paula seemed to have the knack of saying the right thing at the right time. Perhaps that was why she and Fiona had been such close friends for so long.

'Now, come on, what have you found?' Paula asked.

Fiona took down the envelope with Hannah's birth certificate and handed it to Paula.

'Look at the date of birth,' she said.

'First of January 1915. Oh, I see. How unusual. They don't always give times do they?'

'Well, not on my birth certificate, certainly, I had a look.' Fiona replied. 'Did you bring the book?'

Paula reached into her bag and brought out the family history book she had borrowed from the library. She had already looked through the book, so she knew where to find the chapter on birth certificates.

'Here it is,' she said. 'It says here that times of birth are not normally recorded, but there are exceptional reasons why they may be so. One of these is where there is a multiple birth, and another one when the birth takes place on a special day, usually either New Year's Day or Christmas, so that the "First Baby of the New Year", or the "First Baby of Christmas" can be established.'

'She was born on New Year's Day, but it was in the afternoon, 3.10pm it says. So that can't be the reason,' reflected Fiona.

'I'm not sure. It may be that there was a policy of recording all times of birth for babies born on such days. Otherwise it looks as if she must have been a twin then, or even a triplet. But surely you would know if that were the case?' said Paula.

Fiona was thinking.

'I must say I have never noticed on the girls'

certificates, I must have a look. Now Granny Hannah died when I was seventeen, and I used to see quite a lot of her when I was growing up. Her husband Evan had died in the War, and she worked in a factory for many years, I don't know which one now. But I am sure she'd have mentioned it if she were a twin.'

'Maybe the twin died at birth. Would the birth still have been registered if had been a stillbirth?'

'I don't know,' replied Fiona, 'But if the twin had been stillborn there would have been no need to record Granny Hannah's time of birth, would there? What does your book say?'

Paula returned to the book to try to find out what would happen with stillbirths but was unable to find the answer.

'Let's have a look at the list of births for that period,' said Fiona, 'if Hannah were a twin then there would be another Cartwright born at the same time.'

Fiona turned to her computer and searched for the details of Hannah's birth.

'There we are,' she said, 'Hannah Cartwright,

mother's maiden name White, born in the first quarter of 1915, and there is another Cartwright, George, same quarter, same year, same mother's maiden name, same place.'

'So what happened to poor George?' said Paula. 'I suppose he might have died as a child.'

Fiona looked up the death indexes.

'George Cartwright, died aged 0, second quarter of 1915, same place as the birth. I bet that George was Hannah's twin brother.'

This seemed to be fairly conclusive, but to be sure Fiona decided to send for George's birth and death certificates. Having seemingly solved that little problem, Fiona went on to tell Paula about other investigations she was making into her family, and how it was likely there were going to be other finds to surprise her. By the time they had finished their second cup of tea the conversation had strayed to other matters. Paula was anxious about her eldest son's next posting to Afghanistan, and her daughter Jane had taken up with someone at university whom she and her husband Peter thought sounded undesirable, if only from a distance.

Just as Paula stood up to leave the telephone rang. Fiona went across to pick it up and Paula said goodbye. It was Grace.

'Hello, darling,' said Fiona, 'how are things?'

'Fine, thanks Mum. Only we've forgotten something.'

Fiona thought back a few days to that mound in the living room and the car packed so full that you couldn't get anything else in.

'What is it?' she asked, a little more testily than she intended.

'Sorry Mum. You remember Dad asking if we had all our paperwork and we said yes. Well, we didn't.'

'What do you need then?'

'It's registration on Monday and Tuesday next week, and we both need our birth certificates for identification. We could use passports but I think ours are out of date. I thought we had got everything we needed. Can you put them in the post first class? Then we should get them by Tuesday at the latest.'

'Yes, OK. I know where they are. I'll do it straight away. Everything else going well?'

'Yes, Mum. Fine. Thanks. Got to go. Bye.'

Fiona put the phone down. Her girls were clearly enjoying themselves. That was good she told herself. She went to the desk in Michael's office and took out the birth certificates for both girls. She had never looked very closely at them before. Then she noticed something odd. Both girls were born on the same day, same place, same mother and father, but unlike her granny's certificate, there was no time of birth recorded.

But as they were twins why was there no time of birth recorded? Maybe the registrar had just been careless. However as Fiona was sending these off she decided to take copies of both documents so she could study them at her leisure. She put the certificates into the copier and while it churned out the copies she wondered again, and thought how she must speak to

Paula. What a shame she had left when she had. She put the originals into the envelope and walked up the road to post them straight away, but she could not stop thinking about this omission. She thought it might be better not to talk to Michael at the moment; he hadn't been himself ever since he came back from the pub the other night having had a drink with that seed rep. She didn't really know why.

It would have to be Paula.

Fiona worked at Unity Insurance on Wednesdays and Thursdays each week. Working in their claims department she was only a clerk, but as she processed claims from clients she saw the wide array of unfortunate incidents that happened to people, as well as those which didn't, but which people claimed had. Of course, she was not described as a clerk, no one was now, everyone was a customer services advisor, or something similar. The job, however, was the same. Answering the telephone, advising claimants, processing claims and putting customers in touch with tradesmen who would be able to repair or replace lost or broken items. She had worked for Unity for many years and had been part-time since getting married. Seeing all the claims that passed across her desk, although she was not a claims investigator, had given her a feel for claims that were not quite what they said they were. A 'nose' for things that weren't quite right.

It was for this reason that she determined to

telephone Paula later to talk about these birth certificates. She felt sure there must be an innocent explanation, but she could not work out what it was. Talking it over with Paula would help her understand. On arriving home she was caught up doing other things, which delayed her calling her friend. Michael was still behaving curiously. She wondered if he was ill and hadn't told her because it was some dreadful disease that he couldn't come to terms with. Then she dismissed this as stupid. Michael hadn't been to the Doctor's recently, and anyway he was not the type to keep such things from her. It was ever since that meeting with Sam Wainwright that his behaviour seemed to have changed.

After their evening meal Fiona stayed in the kitchen, and Michael went through into the stockroom and office to bring his accounts up-to-date. He was very meticulous in having accurate accounts, and his accountant was appropriately generous when it came to charging him for his end of year accounts. She picked up the telephone and punched in Paula's numbers. She was surprised when Peter answered and said that Paula had gone away for a few days.

'Is everything ok?' she asked.

'Yes, don't worry,' came the reply, 'it's Jane.'

When they had last spoken Paula had told Fiona that Jane had met someone at university whom she thought sounded 'unsavoury'. Peter went on to explain that Jane had been on the phone from a call box earlier in tears, telling her mother about this man, Tom. As Jane was in her second year she was living in a house with five other students in Norwich. She had become very fond of Tom, who was not a student at the University, and he occasionally stayed overnight with her at the house. That morning she woke to find him emptying her handbag of money and plastic cards, and before she could do anything to stop him he had picked up her laptop and mobile and left. She had reported the matter to the Police and to the university authorities, but as he was not a student there was little the university could do. The police were more helpful, and when Jane gave them a description of Tom, they said that they had had a number of similar incidents involving students and someone of his description, but always using a different name. They seemed pessimistic about recovering the stolen items, but said they would let her know if anything happened. Jane suggested to them that it might be a good idea to publicise this man's activities more widely, especially on campus. As a result of this, Paula had travelled up to Norwich that morning, to provide a bit of TLC, but also to advise her daughter to be more careful in future. She would probably not be back before Sunday, ready for working in the shop on Monday.

Fiona expressed her sympathies and put the phone down. She could either wait for Paula's return or do a bit of investigative work herself. Or she could speak to Michael. She got out the certificates again and looked at them.

'Grace Downing, mother Louise Downing formerly Baxter, father Michael Downing, bookseller, born 5 March 1993 at 14 Clayton Road, Emberton, registered by Michael Downing, father.'

'Victoria Downing – details identical.'

While thinking about these births, Fiona decided to do more work towards the folders for the girls. It would be useful to have a note of the exact date when Michael and Louise had married because she would then be able to annotate photographs with dates and places. She felt as if she was going behind Michael's back doing this, but she rationalised that by saying to herself that the end result would be worth it. She went back to the Internet to search for Michael and Louise's marriage. She decided to start in March 1993 and work backwards. Just as she was keying in the details Michael came through the door, and came up behind her. Looking over her shoulder he could see the copies of the girls' birth certificates.

'What's all this then?' he said. 'Finding out my secrets?'

He smiled as he said the words; that smile which he knew Fiona loved him for.

'I was just doing something for the girls,' Fiona replied, 'I thought I would put together a folder of photographs, dates and a family tree for them. Now they are grown up I think they ought to know more about their birth mother, so I copied their birth certificates and I was going to get a copy of your marriage certificate and put it with some photos of you and Louise for them. I wanted to do it as a surprise for you as well, so I was just going to search for your marriage details when you came in.'

'Well,' he said, ' there is a bit of a story and you might have had difficulty finding the marriage details. When Louise got pregnant we were not married.'

He held up his hand to stop her.

'I know, I know, that doesn't seem like such a big deal now, or maybe even then, but Louise wanted to be married before the girls were born. Then I lost my job at the library where I worked, we had all the business of selling the house, buying the business, moving and there just wasn't time. Then the girls were born, a few days before we moved. We had planned to marry and did so almost immediately we got here. Before we moved I went to register the girl's births and I told the registrar that we were already married, and gave Louise's name as Downing. Probably shouldn't have done but who knows now? It's not really important.'

'Now I know your secret I shan't tell anyone. But there is one thing that puzzles me. Paula's book about family history says that with twins the times of birth are always recorded, but there is nothing on Grace's or Victoria's.'

'I must say I can't remember, It was eighteen years ago. Maybe he just forgot to ask me, I don't know. Anyway Louise and I were married on 14 April 1993 in the Register Office here.'

Michael walked out of the kitchen and back into his office. As he did so Fiona keyed in the details to search for a Downing getting married. There it was, April 1993. A few moments later Michael returned with a green piece of paper.

'There you are. All legal now,' he said as he handed Fiona the marriage certificate. There it was, Louise Baxter, spinster, bookseller, father Edward Baxter, schoolteacher, marrying Michael Downing, bachelor, bookseller, father James Downing, postman, deceased, on 14 April 1993 at Hopley Register Office.

'Can I take copies of this for the girls' folder?'

'Yes, of course,' Michael said, 'in fact, I'll do it for you.'

As he came back into the room with the copies, Fiona put her arms around him and kissed him. It was, perhaps, a kiss of relief as much as anything.

Paula returned from Norwich on the Saturday and when Peter told her of his conversation with Fiona she rang her straight away.

'How is Jane now?'

Fiona asked anxiously when she answered the phone.

'Better now. I think she's learned a lesson, a hard one, for sure. But I think she'll be more careful in future.'

'Do the police think they will catch him?'

'Probably not. They are going to put posters up around the university to warn other students. Bit late, though, really. Jane and I went out into Norwich to replace the things she's lost; plastic cards, NUS card and so on. It's all such a performance though. Sorry, Fi, you must hear this every day at work.'

'Yes, it does sound familiar. At least she was sensible enough to have insurance. So often students think that their possessions are covered on Mum and Dad's insurance at home, and it's not always the case; that's when we get cross customers.'

'Any progress with your family history? Found any secrets out about Granny Hannah?'

'No. I have sent for George's death certificate, but I am not expecting any great revelations there. But, remember when you were last here and just as you were leaving the phone rang and it was Grace?'

'Yes.'

'She asked me to send both their birth certificates for their registration day at the university, and that was when I spotted something odd.'

Fiona explained about the lack of times on the twins' certificates, and the subsequent conversation with Michael, including the story of his marriage to Louise.

'It does sound a bit strange, but it's ok now, isn't it?' said Paula.

'I suppose so. Just seems a bit funny, that's all. You're probably right; I don't know what I must have been thinking. Anyway, now I've told Michael about the folder I can continue without too much worry, and if necessary I can ask him for details'

Fiona felt easier having spoken both to Michael and Paula. She could foresee no further problems with her plans for the twins.

Chapter Eight

A stiff October breeze and a spattering of rain kept the door to the bookshop closed. Michael had always been an outdoor person, what with his athletics and tennis, and he liked to keep the shop door open whenever possible. Fiona was just the opposite, with the door closed and heaters on she preferred to be cosy. The town was looking grey and sad. Christmas was only on the horizon, but summer was long gone. It would be November next week and the Christmas lights in the town would be strung up between the lamp posts on the high street. Each day saw more Christmas stock arrive, both Michael and other high street shops eager to ensnare the Christmas shopper. He would soon be decorating the shop for the season, but did not want to be too premature; he thought it put people off to see fairy lights before Bonfire Night.

Life had settled into a comfortable routine since Grace and Victoria had left. He was gearing up for Christmas now, but also looking forward to the girls' return. Fiona was engrossed in her folder project which she was hoping to be able to give to the twins at Christmas. The telephone rang and he answered it with his usual greeting.

'Good morning, Hopley Bookshop. How can I help you?'

'Hello, Dad,'

Victoria's familiar voice was at the other end.

'Hello, darling. How are you both?'

'Fine, thanks. We're coming home this weekend if that's ok. I tried ringing Mum but no one's answering the home phone.'

'That's because she's at work. You've forgotten already,' he said, laughing. 'Do you need picking up?'

'Just from the station, Friday, three minutes past six the train arrives.'

'Lovely. One of us will be there.'

'Bye, Dad.'

These conversations never seemed to last very long, Michael thought. Still, all must be well or we would have heard. He remembered the upset with Jane Hamilton only a week or so ago and an old song came to mind, Who sang it? Perry Como? How long ago was that? But how true.

Fiona was pleased when she came home to the news that the girls were coming home for the weekend.

'I'll cook something special for them. They're probably not feeding themselves properly. You go and pick them up, and I'll have it ready on your return.'

Friday was busy Michael was pleased to see, as the rest of the week, with the awful weather, had been dire. The shop normally closed at 5.30pm, but if there were still customers in at that time Michael let them stay, hoping they would buy something, which they usually did. As he was anxious to close promptly to give him time to get to the station he was slightly disappointed to still have people in the shop at 5.30pm. However, they left shortly afterwards, and just as he was locking the front door, he heard a familiar voice.

'Hello, Mike,' it squeaked.

He looked across the road to see the overweight shape of Sam Wainwright.

'Fancy a drink tonight? I'm passing through, thought we could have a quick word. I'm staying at the Waggon like before. Eight OK?'

Michael was already pleased that Grace and Victoria were coming home, now he was even more pleased.

'No, sorry Sam, can't. Got the family coming home. I'm just off to pick them up. Got to go.'

'Shame. Ah well, maybe next time. I've been thinking about what we spoke about last time.
I should be back before Christmas, but it's not a very busy time right now. If so I'll see you then.'

Michael was relieved to lock the door, close the till and shut down everything for the day. After a few moments of reflection he walked back through to the back door to pick up the car. As he drove down towards the station he tried not to think too much about that conversation in the pub.
He really did not want to meet Sam Wainwright again.

Michael parked at the station at two minutes past six. While he was waiting two attractive young women came out of the station and walked across in his direction. I wonder if the train is on time, he wondered, surely they would have rung if it was going to be late. The knock on the window of the car made him jump. He turned and saw the two women who had just walked across the car park.

'I didn't recognise you,' he said, almost embarrassed to have not noticed his own daughters. He made the excuse that it was the new hairstyles and different clothes, but he knew it was that in those few short weeks the girls who had left home had grown into young women, and he thought it was wonderful. He hugged them both and put their bags in the boot. Who was it they reminded him of he mused, as he drove back to the flat. These pleasant thoughts were interrupted by thoughts of Sam, which he tried to put to the back of his mind.

Fiona was ready with a splendid roast joint of beef, with all the expected accompaniments, which she knew was the girls' favourite. Her roast dinners had acquired her something of a reputation among their friends also. When everything had been cleared away they sat down together to hear all the news. Grace and

Victoria were full of details about other students, boys and girls, fellow hall residents, tutors, accommodation, everything except work. When pressed, they both said that the work was going well and they had had good marks for the initial work they had handed in.

Fiona told them about Jane Hamilton's unfortunate experience, and Grace said that a girl on another landing had told a story about someone she knew who had fallen into a similar trap. Both Fiona and Michael expressed their worry about either of the girls getting caught in this way, and both Grace and Victoria assured them they had no cause for concern. Victoria said she would like to help out in the shop in the morning, so that she could see as many people as possible. Michael said he would be very happy for her to do that, but in his heart he hoped that Sam would not put in an appearance.

As the girls were going up to bed Fiona hugged each one of them, just a little tighter than usual, and said how good it was to have them at home. Michael smiled a smile of contentment as he noticed this, but said nothing.

The next day Victoria's time in the shop passed without incident. She saw many people she knew, and told them excitedly about her new life. Regular customers noticed, as Michael had, how much more grown up Victoria was after just a few weeks away. She was becoming quite a beauty. Grace and Fiona went shopping; shopping was always Grace's weakness, and having bought one or two essentials, and a number of extravagances financed by Grace's student loan, they called in on Paula and Peter to see how Jane was now. Paula told them that she was fine now, and she was sure there would be no repeat of that episode. The police had not caught up with the culprit, but Jane had submitted an insurance claim for her losses, obtained new plastic cards and was keen to put the whole thing behind her.

The weekend was very enjoyable for all concerned and on Sunday afternoon Michael took the twins back to the station for the 4.10pm train. He looked at their small cases which they had brought home for the weekend, as they prepared to leave.

'Not like last time then,' he joked, as he caught the girls' eyes.

'Just wait for the summer,' Victoria replied, 'you'll need a big lorry by then.'

Fiona smiled at this exchange. Michael had such an easy rapport with the girls, it was clear he loved them both very much. As they said goodbye, Fiona told Grace and Victoria that she was planning a special Christmas present for them, which left the girls intrigued, but she was saying no more.

'Two youngsters made a grisly discovery as they were walking home from school this afternoon through Hartstone Woods on the outskirts of Emberton.'

The television news was chattering away in the background in the kitchen as Fiona prepared the evening meal. She was not really paying attention until this item came up, and the name of Emberton was mentioned. The report continued;

'On their way home from school two eleven-year old boys were playing in Hartstone Woods, near Emberton, when they discovered what appeared to be human remains in a shallow grave. Inspector Charles Burton of Emberton CID said there had been some storm damage in the woods recently resulting in trees being brought down. It seems that the uprooted trees revealed a grave, which had then been further disturbed by wild animals, possibly foxes. He went on to say that the boys had been very sensible in calling 999 on their mobile. He said he had no further information at present, but forensic tests would be undertaken to establish, if possible, the age, sex and identity of the body.'

Michael walked into the kitchen part way through the report, and sat and listened intently.

'Hartstone Woods. That takes me back. Popular place for "courting couples" as they used to be called. Had my first kiss in Hartstone. Pretty girl, Sandra, her name was. Mind you, I was only 12 at the time. Wonder what happened to her? Wrinkled old granny by now.'

'Michael!' Fiona exclaimed. 'She's your age, I expect. How would you like it if someone described you as 'some old boy'?'

Michael looked suitably chastened.

'Sorry. Bit of a shock hearing something like that though. Wonder who she was?'

'How do you know it was a she? Could be anyone.'

'Yes, I suppose so,' Michael replied, 'somehow

you always imagine bodies buried in woods are women. Men are buried under motorway bridges.'

'Rubbish. Too much TV crime, that's your trouble.'

'Was that national or local news?' Michael asked.

'Only local. Not important enough for national yet. Might graduate, depending on what the police discover.'

Michael and Fiona sat down to eat. Fiona was a good cook and now she did not have to worry about the twins' likes and dislikes she could experiment more, and Michael was a willing participant in these experiments. They were both very fond of fish and shellfish, and tonight Fiona had cooked herrings, coated with oatmeal and mustard and then grilled, followed by zabaglione.

'How are the folders coming on?' Michael asked.

'Fine, but I could do with some photos of you with Louise, and also with your Mum and Dad if you have any. All the ones I can find are of us, when the children are growing up. Baby ones would be nice.'

Fiona did not say so, but she was also going to try to get copies of Michael's parents' marriage and birth certificates, but she could order these online without his involvement.

'I think I know where there might be some. I'll sort them out for you.'

A day or so later Michael and Fiona were watching the local news when there was a further report on the find in Hartstone Woods.

'Emberton CID has issued a further statement today about the discovery earlier this week of an unidentified body in Hartstone Woods near Emberton. The body is said to be that of a female, aged approximately forty years, and who may have been dead for as long as twenty years. Further forensic tests are being undertaken to determine identity and cause of death.'

'Maybe it's Sandra,' said Michael, 'died of a

broken heart after I left.'

'Michael! Stop it! It's not funny. That woman was someone's daughter, and may have been someone's mother, wife or sister. How can you be so horrible?'

'Sorry. No, I know it wasn't her. She married a lorry driver and went to live in Scotland.'

'It might have been around the time you left Emberton, though. Do you remember any reports of missing people on the news at the time?'

'No, can't remember. Mind you, these things come and go very quickly, don't they? We all think about them briefly and then seem to forget them just as easily.'

Sam Wainwright poured himself another beer. He had been on the road as a rep now for just over two years, and it was getting him down. Week after week of hotel rooms, and cheap ones at that, did little for the waistline and even less for the social life. He was out of touch with most of his friends from Emberton since he had divorced his wife, and financially he was having difficulty making ends meet.

This week he was in Reading, but it might as well have been Basingstoke, Winchester, Swindon or any other town across the south and south Midlands. He put the television on, not really expecting to be interested in what was on, more for something to do until he drank himself to sleep.

'Emberton CID has issued a further statement today about the discovery this week of an unidentified body in Hartstone Woods near Emberton on Tuesday. The body is said to be that of a female, aged approximately forty years, and who may have been dead for as long as twenty years. Further forensic tests are being undertaken to determine identity and cause of death.'

Sam sat bolt upright. Did he hear that item correctly? He flicked through the newspaper he had bought. The news he had on at the moment was BBC local news. Maybe he could catch the news on another channel, and check what he had just heard and seen. There it was; in half an hour's time on ITV was their regional news. He must watch. He changed channels so that he was ready for it, and settled back on the bed. When he awoke he looked at the clock by the bed, 12.45am; the television was showing an old episode of That was the last thing he wanted to watch. Annoyed with himself for falling asleep at the wrong moment, he turned the television off and got undressed and ready for bed.

'I must get a paper tomorrow. I bet I know who that is.'

He smiled to himself, because if he was right, he would not be ringing the police, but quite a different number.

The following morning Sam did not go downstairs for breakfast before setting off on his calls for the day. There was some more important work to be done. He went out of the hotel and along the street to a little newsagent where he bought a copy of every newspaper he could find. He returned to his room, made himself a coffee and sat on the bed. He spread the newspapers across the bed and scanned the pages of each one, leaving his coffee to go cold in his eagerness. All the papers were nationals, and unfortunately most of them carried nothing of the story at all. Only two, and had small articles, which told him no more than the television news had. He opened his laptop, logged on and searched the news websites with an equal lack of success. Disappointed, he told himself he must keep watching the television news and reading the papers, there were bound to be developments soon, and he wanted to be ready.

Fiona was keen to return to her family tree building, and over the coming days she searched for her own ancestors, on both sides of her family. The Evans strand was proving very difficult and she was thankful that on the Welsh side she had not discovered anyone with the name of Jones. She thought that would be completely hopeless, considering the number she had come across just casually. As she made further progress she decided she should buy some computer software which she had seen advertised, which would help her to keep everyone in the right place with regard to each other. She knew that the computer shop in town stocked this software and as she was walking down the road to the shop she met Paula, who invited her for a drink at the local coffee shop. Fiona readily agreed and they went into the Beans'n'Leaves and took a seat. Paula ordered a coffee for her and a pot of tea for Fiona.

'What news, then?'

Paula was keen to learn of Fiona's progress. Fiona brought her up to date and then Paula mentioned the Emberton body.

'That was what I wanted to see you about really,' Paula said, 'do you, or Michael more accurately, know anything about it?'

'No, I certainly don't. Michael knows the area, of course; says he, like lots of other people, used the woods for what he quaintly described as "courting".

Said he had his first kiss there. He doesn't remember anyone going missing around that time. It might be after he left, though. There's no definitive date on when she was buried there. Michael and Louise came here to Hopley in March 1993, so they might have just missed it.'

exciting

'How's Danny now?' Fiona enquired, anxious to change the subject. 'Has he got a date for Afghanistan yet?'

'Probably after Christmas. Either he's not sure or he just isn't telling us. I must say I'm worried about the prospect. Although it was always going to come, I suppose I tried to put it out of my mind. Joseph is doing well, but Jane has still not recovered from that business with Tom. She's very careful about making new friends and going to new places, I think that is hampering her.'

'I came out to buy one of those family tree computer programmes; otherwise I think it will start to be too much for me to keep track of everyone. I've been making good progress on my family, and I need to put it all together in some sort of order. I also need to find out more about Michael's parents and particularly their background. When I have entered everything in, come and have a look and we will see if we can fill the gaps. I'm becoming quite obsessive about it, it pulls you in.'

'I can see that,' Paula said. 'I shall look forward to seeing the fruits of your labours.'

Paula drank the dregs of her coffee and stood up to leave. Fiona did likewise, and then suddenly stopped and turned to Paula.

'You do think Michael is all right, don't you?' she said

'Yes, of course. Don't be silly. Why shouldn't he be?' Paula replied.

'Nothing. Just...' Fiona's sentence tailed off as she realised how silly she was being.

'Bye, Paula, I'll ring you.'

Paula left the café feeling slightly disturbed at Fiona's comment

The Emberton body made the national news that evening as there had been further developments. Fiona was sitting at her computer filling in the details on the new software as the reporter gave the outline of the discoveries so far. She was not listening very closely until the newsreader said that the body had a gunshot wound to the head. There was still no confirmation of the identity, but Inspector Burton, who had spoken on the case before, said that it was now a murder enquiry. He reaffirmed the likely age and sex of the body, and said that DNA testing would hopefully provide a definite identity. In the meantime he urged anyone who had any knowledge of a woman of that age going missing in the Emberton area twenty years ago, to get in touch with him or his team.

Immediately the report had finished the telephone rang.

'Fiona.' It was Paula. 'Have you just seen the news?'

'Yes, I have.'

'What did you mean when you said that to me in the café this afternoon?'

'Just me being silly, forget it. But on other matters, I've never seen any photographs of Michael before he married Louise, except some baby ones with his parents and his brother. Michael was over forty when he married Louise and I know virtually nothing about him before that. I'd never thought about it until I started this family tree business. Do you think that is odd, or am I worrying about something which isn't there?'

'I'm sure everything is ok, you're worrying over nothing.'

Paula wanted to console her friend and offer some sensible advice, but was finding it difficult. As Fiona was at work the following two days there was little Paula could do, but she kept thinking about what Fiona had said, and it concerned her.

Fiona put the phone down and turned back to her computer. She was keying in the details of Michael and Louise's marriage when she realised she needed the marriage index register number for the new software she had bought. She looked it up again on the website, and there it was, Michael Downing marrying Louise Baxter in April 1993. But then her eye caught sight of another Downing at the top of the page. What was this? A Michael Downing marrying a Deborah Roberts. She looked at the detailed entry. Michael Downing marrying Deborah Roberts in Emberton in June 1987.

She froze.

Then, regaining her senses, she printed the page and left the website.

Sam Wainwright was in Andover this week, another anonymous hotel on his round of anonymous hotels. He seemed to spend so little of his time at his flat in Emberton it hardly seemed worthwhile keeping it on. But he had to have somewhere to spend the weekends, even if it was only somewhere to drink himself to sleep in an effort to forget the disaster his life had become. Since his divorce his ex-wife had remarried and he saw her around the town occasionally. Last time he saw her she was very pregnant, and he wondered if children might have made any difference. Too late now. Still, there was hope of an improvement in his situation if Michael Downing played ball. He had been doing what he had promised himself, buying the papers every day, watching the news, searching the internet, and now he had been rewarded. A piece on the national news, giving the full details about the Emberton body inquiry, and requesting help from members of the public who might have information as to missing persons from that area and era. Maybe the finances were about to take a turn for the better, he thought.

Each year Michael went to one of the trade shows put on by the major book wholesalers which showcased the up-and-coming titles for Christmas. This gave him the opportunity not only to see the books before buying them, as opposed to buying from a catalogue or a rep's recommendations, but it also enabled him to meet with other booksellers in a similar situation to his own. These shows usually took place in October, and this year Michael had not been able to attend, and he was disappointed at missing out. Hopley Bookshop had been a good and regular customer of one book wholesaler for many years and Michael had established a friendly relationship with many of the staff. As he had been unable to attend the show this year the company suggested that he went to visit them for the day, giving him opportunity to catch up with what he had missed out on the previous month. So on Wednesday, 12th November, Michael set off early to travel to Birmingham where the wholesaler was based. As it was a Wednesday, Fiona was working at Unity, and Michael had arranged for

Paula to work an extra day, which she was delighted to do. Fiona had not had the chance to pursue her investigations into the marriage details she had uncovered, nor had she been able to speak to Paula.

Trade in the shop was steadily increasing as Christmas approached and plans for presents were being formulated. Customers would very often browse around and perhaps make enquiries, then leave, writing down details of books they hoped other people would buy them at Christmas. The morning passed quickly. Paula hurriedly ate her lunch in a lull. The telephone rang and she answered promptly as Michael had taught her.

'Good afternoon, Hopley Bookshop, how can I help you?'

'Can I speak to Michael Downing please?'

It did not sound like a junk call from someone offering to sell insurance or advertising, but then, it did not sound like a customer either. If the customers knew Michael they would say, 'Can I speak to Michael?' or if they did not, they would not use a name at all.

'Who's speaking please?'

'I need to speak to Michael Downing. Is he there please? Is that his wife?'

Paula became more defensive. Who was this person, and why should they think she was his wife?

'Michael Downing is not here today. I am not his wife, but I am looking after the business in Mr Downing's absence.'

She sensed the irritation at the other end of the line. The voice became more conciliatory.

'Sorry about that. I didn't mean to sound brusque. My name is Sam Wainwright and I'm a sales rep with Harpers Seeds.'

Paula frowned. Why was a seed salesman ringing Michael in such a manner?

'When I was in Hopley a month or so ago I called into the bookshop to buy a map, and when I was there Mike and I realised we knew each other from a long time ago.'

Paula frowned again. No-one calls Michael Mike. What is this all about?

'We knew each other when Mike lived in Emberton,' Sam continued, 'he and I were members of the same athletics club, the Emberton Runners. He was quite a bit older than me. He used to supervise a lot of my training.'

Paula's interest was now growing. She knew that Michael had lived in Emberton prior to coming to Hopley, and Fiona had mentioned to her once that Michael was keen on running. However, she had never met anyone who knew Michael from those days, except Louise, of course. She was feeling friendlier towards Sam now, and intrigued as well. With Fiona doing her family history project for the girls she thought Sam could be useful to her, filling in some background. She had said only the other day that she knew little about Michael before Hopley. It was her turn to apologise.

'Sorry, Mr Wainwright.'

'Sam, please.'

'Sorry, Sam. It's just that we get so many calls from people who are just trying to sell something. I have to be a little bit careful'

Well I do have something to sell, but not what you might think, Sam thought to himself.

'That's ok, I understand,' Sam said, 'but I would like to speak to Mike. We had an interesting chat last time I came to Hopley, and something's cropped up I wanted to ask him about.'

'Can I help, or maybe give him a message?'

Paula was eager to help because she hoped she might find out something for Fiona.

Sam hesitated. He was not certain how much to say, but he had plucked up courage to make this call; he did not want to waste the opportunity, although he knew he would have to speak to him in person as well. He decided that he would ask her to pass a message on to Michael.

'It was about his first wife,' Sam said, 'when I came to Hopley last time we had a chat about her in the pub.'

'Louise, you mean. She was killed in a car crash.'

'Yes, I know that. No, we were talking about before her. Deborah; gave him a hard time as far I understand. Mean with the cash, or so people tell me. Kept him on a tight rein. Bit of a looker, though, dark hair and curves in all the right places. Didn't seem to work, though. Anyway, tell Mike I'll come and see him next time I'm in Hopley. Should be before Christmas. Bye.'

Sam put the phone down and poured himself a large scotch from the bottle he had treated himself to that morning. Shame he wasn't there, he thought, still, I'm sure the message will get through. Wonder who she was? Another notch on his bedpost?

Sam took another drink, looked at the clock, then back at the bottle. He decided to finish the rest tonight. It was well into the afternoon, and if he did not make a move soon and get out to his customers he would be losing this job, and then he would need the money even more.

As the telephone clicked down at Sam's end, the shop door opened and a young family came in, followed by a middle-aged couple. Paula was busy for most of the afternoon, but her thoughts kept going back to the conversation with this Sam. She wondered how much Fiona knew about him, and what, if anything, she knew about Deborah. Michael would not be back from Birmingham until later in the evening, he was being taken out to dinner by the company, and so, unusually, Paula rang Fiona at work.

'Unity Insurance, Claims Department, Fiona speaking, how can I help you today?'

Fiona hated this preamble, and was sure customers were not keen on it either, but the company insisted.

'Fi, it's me. Something has come up. Can I see you tonight?'

'Oh, hello Paula. Yes, of course. Why don't we have a takeaway? Michael's out till late, I've got something to tell you which I am a bit worried about. I need your wise advice.'

'Good idea about the takeaway, I'll bring it with me.'

Paula did not need to ask Fiona what she wanted as it was always the same. She did not tell

Fiona about Sam's call either, better to do that face-to-face. She telephoned the local Indian restaurant and ordered three meals. She picked them up after shutting up the shop, and went back home, dropping off the madras curry for Peter, and then she made her way back across town to Fiona's. When she arrived she saw that Fiona had opened a bottle of wine and they sat and ate their meal, washed down with a couple of glasses of red, chatting about nothing in particular. The subjects that both of them wanted to raise were too important not to give full concentration to. After they had finished, Fiona made Paula a coffee, herself a pot of tea, and they sat down with Fiona's computer switched on alongside them.

Michael's day had been a good one. He had the chance to view most of the new Christmas titles, and place orders for them at advantageous rates; he had a good lunch in the company restaurant with the staff he knew (Michael thought it was much too good to be called a canteen), and then had been wined and dined by the Sales Director in the evening. As he was going to be driving home he was careful about what he had to drink, and at half past nine he set off on the two hour journey back to Hopley. As he was driving along the M42 there was a worrying noise from under the bonnet, and although Michael was no mechanic he recognised a noise that sounded expensive, if not terminal. He pulled over to the hard shoulder and called the AA. Thank goodness he had kept up the membership. When he had bought the Toyota from Fiona's Dad's garage he had been tempted to give up his membership. When he had raised the possibility of something going wrong with the car David Lewis had said;

'Don't be silly, Michael. It's a Toyota.'

With that advice he could so easily have cancelled his AA membership. He was pleased he had listened to his own advice, and not a car salesman's. The mechanic arrived 25 minutes later, shortly after a visit from the motorway police who had stopped to check that all was well. After a brief examination of the engine the AA mechanic said that it would need garage attention, and called up a tow-truck to take

Michael and his stricken car home. In the meantime Michael rang Fiona and told her what had happened, and said it would be well after twelve before he was home. As he had a key with him he suggested she went to bed and did not wait up for him. Fiona told him that Paula had come over for the evening so there was no need to worry about her. Michael was pleased with that and waited for the AA to get the car loaded, and then he travelled home in the front of the van, gently snoozing.

'I'm worried about Michael.'

Fiona and Paula had finished their takeaway and were sitting in the kitchen, Paula ensconced in her usual chair, and Fiona at the table looking at her computer screen.

'What in particular?' asked Paula, not at this point wanting to raise the subject of Sam's call.

'It's ever since the visit from that seed rep, Sam, I think his name is. He's been irritable and on edge. Snaps my head off as soon as I look at him. He never used to be like that. I don't know what he said to him, but it has certainly had an effect.'

'Who is he?' asked Paula, testing how much Fiona already knew about this man.

'I think Michael knew him before coming here. They were members of the same athletics club, I believe. I don't really know any more than that. Only that from the way Michael has been behaving, it would seem as if he has some sort of hold over him. Goodness knows what.'

'Have you asked him?' Paula said.

'Not really. He seems very sensitive on the subject so I have tended to keep away from it. Trouble is, ever since I have been doing this family tree folder, one or two things have come up which have set me thinking. Look at this.'

Fiona took out the printout of the marriage index that showed a Michael Downing having married a Deborah Roberts back in 1987.

'What do you make of that? Michael doesn't know I have found this, and it might not be my Michael, but if it is why does he describe himself as a bachelor when he marries Louise?'

She showed Paula a copy of Michael and Louise's marriage certificate. Fiona took out the copies of the twins' birth certificates which she had made.

'He told me he lied on these. He said that he and Louise were not married when they were born, but he told the registrar they were to save Louise any embarrassment. I suppose if you can lie on one certificate you can lie on another. But who is this

Deborah Roberts?'

'Why don't you send for the Downing/Roberts marriage certificate? Until then you don't really know, unless you want to ask him which I assume you don't, whether we are talking about the same Michael Downing.'

'Thanks Paula,' said Fiona, 'I know you are trying to be positive, but you don't really think there are two Michael Downings getting married in Emberton, do you?'

Paula thought back to her earlier conversation with Sam Wainwright and decided she knew the answer to that question, but that would keep for the moment.

'Maybe he was married before, she died, or they got divorced, and Michael has never wanted to admit to it. Can you look up to see if a Deborah Downing has died in the time between 1987 and when he married Louise?'

'Yes, I can. Let's have a look.'

Fiona checked the deaths between 1987 and 1993. There were none, as she had expected.

'Divorced?' suggested Paula.

'Can't check such things so recent. I'd have to ask him, but I can hardly do that.'

'Fi,' said Paula, hesitantly, 'I had a phone call today at the shop.'

'Oh yes; is that what you wanted to talk to me about? I wondered when we were going to get to that. Jane again? Don't tell me she's done it again?'

'Goodness me, no, I don't think she will ever fall into that trap again. No, it is to do with Michael.'

Fiona looked agitated.

'What?'

'It was just after lunch today. It was that seed rep, Sam. Said he wanted to speak to Michael. I said I would give him a message, and he said to tell Michael he would see him when he came to Hopley next time.'

'Michael said that he thought he'd be in touch again, but what's the big deal?'

'He told me he wanted to speak about Michael's first wife, and I told him Louise was dead. He said he knew that, but he wanted to talk about before that. He said that he knew Michael was married before Louise, to a woman named Deborah, who was a "bit of a looker" as he described her. He said, at least according to what someone had told him, that she gave Michael a hard time, and was mean with money. I wonder if he was just fishing, because he didn't have much detail apart from knowing about the marriage, just what other people had told him. Of course it meant nothing when he said that name to me, but this now puts it in a different light.'

Fiona looked shocked.

'So this Sam is saying that Michael was married to Deborah before Louise, that he was unhappy, and that he wants to speak to Michael about it. Why would he want to do that? What does he know?'

'Nothing I should think,' said Paula, 'Just a chancer making wild guesses.'

'But Michael was married to Deborah; so what happened?'

Fiona's face suddenly went white.

'Have you seen the news recently? The Emberton body. No surely not.'

Paula put her arms around Fiona.

'Don't be silly.'

'What's the latest on that? Let's put the news on.'

Fiona went across to the television and switched it on. The BBC news was just beginning. There was the usual summary of world events, followed by a headline that said there had been developments in the Emberton body case. Fiona and Paula waited anxiously for the programme to reach that item of news.

'Emberton CID announced today that the previously unidentified body of a woman found in woodland near the town three weeks ago has now been confirmed to be that of Sally Mitchell, a forty-one year old former prostitute. Ms Mitchell went missing in Chatham in Kent in early 1993, and she has been identified by DNA analysis of specimens taken when she had been arrested and charged for drug offences in 1992. Tests on the remains found at Hartstone Woods are consistent with those specimens. As far as the police are aware she had no previous connection with the Emberton area. They are appealing for anyone who had any dealings with Ms Mitchell in 1993 to contact them.'

Fiona collapsed in tears.

'Thank goodness for that. I couldn't really imagine Michael shooting anybody, but with all that has gone on recently.'

Paula put her arms around her again.

'Let's just wait for that marriage certificate, shall we?'

She poured Fiona another glass of wine.

'Come on, get this down you, and then get to bed. You've had quite enough for one day.'

Fiona wiped her tears away and gulped down the drink.

'Thanks, Paula. I don't know what I would do without you.'

'I've got a husband at home who has probably finished watching the football and is wondering where I've got to. Don't you worry any more, go on, up to bed.'

Fiona nodded, and as Paula put her coat on to leave she started to tidy up before going upstairs.

'Thanks, Paula. I'll ring when I have more news.'

Sam was feeling pleased with himself. He had sown enough seeds of doubt in that woman's mind and was sure they would be passed on to Michael. Patience was all he needed. He turned the television on; the news was halfway through.

'...confirmed to be that of Sally Mitchell, a forty-one year old former prostitute. Ms Mitchell went missing in Chatham in Kent in early 1993 and she has been identified by DNA analysis of specimens taken when she had been arrested and charged for drug offences in 1990. Tests on the remains found at Hartstone Woods are consistent with those specimens. As far as the police are aware she had no previous connection with the Emberton area. They are appealing for anyone who had any dealings with Ms Mitchell in 1993 to contact them.'

He switched off the television in disgust and stared in disbelief. His plan was in ruins. He could have done with the money which he had hoped was going to be coming his way, but not even he thought he could blackmail Michael Downing over the death of a prostitute twenty years ago. He looked across the room; the bottle of Scotch stared back at him, two-thirds full.

Might as well drown my sorrows as celebrate, he thought, picking up a plastic beaker and pouring the whisky into it. In a short space of time the bottle was empty. Sam lay on the bed, and watched the ceiling gradually spinning around. He had been a heavy drinker for some time now and it was a feeling he had grown used to. He tried to sit up and swayed sideways, as he did so he steadied himself on the edge of the bed and a pain shot through his left arm. He grasped his arm with his other arm and toppled off the bed on to the floor. Struggling to get up, he knocked the bedside lamp and broke the shade, the plastic splintering across the floor. He felt as if a vice were clamped to his chest and he slumped back on to the bed. He pulled at the neck of his shirt, trying to get more air. He gasped and gasped for more air, but the pain of breathing was too much. Sam lost consciousness, for the last time.

The following morning there was no noise from room 26. Nor was there an occupant of room 26 at breakfast, although that was not especially unusual. However, later the same morning the chambermaid could not gain access to the room and, despite several attempts, she was unable to make contact with Mr Wainwright, to whom she had spoken the day before, and whom she knew from previous visits. She went downstairs to the manager's office, and called Mr Spinks, who was the duty Manager for the day.

'Ted, I can't get into room 26.' she said.

'Who's in there? That Wainwright chap?' replied Ted Spinks, irritated at being interrupted from looking at the latest offering on Page Three.

'Yes, and he's not answering. I'm worried about him.'

'Ok, Lianne. I'll come up with the pass key'

Ted Spinks and Lianne walked back upstairs together. When they reached the door of room 26 Spinks called out.

'Mr Wainwright, can you let me in?'

There was no answer. Spinks knocked on the door and called again. Again there was no answer. He put the pass key in the lock and opened the door. Walking in to the room they both saw Sam Wainwright sprawled across the bed, his face distorted in a grimace of pain, his hand grasping at his throat in a final effort to breathe. His lips were blue and his eyes bloodshot and staring. Lianne screamed. Spinks put his arms around her in a fatherly way and dried her tears.

'You just go downstairs and ask Marie to make you a hot cup of tea.'

Having sent Lianne downstairs Spinks picked up the telephone in the room and dialled 999.

'Police and Ambulance please,' he said authoritatively, 'The Bear Hotel, Andover. We have a dead resident; at least he looks dead.'

Spinks put the phone down and looked again at

the body, and noticed the empty whisky bottle on the side. Alongside the bottle he saw some press cuttings about a body being discovered in Emberton, screwed up as if ready to be thrown away. He put them in the bin and walked out of the room, locking it behind him. He went back to his office downstairs and awaited the arrival of the police. He smiled inwardly; this was the most exciting thing to happen to him in a long time. Shame about Wainwright. Still, who was he? Another sad nonentity in an anonymous hotel room. Who cared?

Fiona washed up the few bits of crockery left over after Paula's visit. She walked upstairs and got ready for bed. Michael wouldn't be home for hours yet, she thought. She got into bed and she started to drift away in sleep, the wine taking effect. Suddenly she sat up with a start.

She had been so relieved to learn that the Emberton body was nothing to do with Michael, but now her concerns turned back to the mystery of Deborah Roberts. If the Emberton body was not

Deborah, which she had feared, then the answer must lie elsewhere. Michael had been so tense when the name of Sam Wainwright had been mentioned, and it was clearly nothing to do with Sally Mitchell. Therefore there must be something else that this man knows about Michael that is causing him concern. The more she thought about it the more she thought it must have something to do with this marriage certificate she was waiting to receive. She would just have to be patient, and hopefully that would provide the answer. If when it came it did not, asking Michael for an explanation seemed to be the only solution.

She reached out an arm as she lay down again, she did not like being on her own in bed, with that big space alongside her. She felt chilly and wanted to be warm.

Upon Michael's return Fiona said nothing of her discoveries about a Downing/Roberts marriage, or Sam Wainwright's phone call. In truth, she was reluctant to think of her husband as anything but the loving husband he had always been to her. She was constantly hoping for a different explanation from the obvious one, because the obvious one was not very palatable. So she wanted to wait for the certificate to arrive before she made her next move. Since starting her family history quest, she had come to realise that there were often many people with the same name, very often in the same town. However, remembering what Sam had said made this most unlikely.

Michael had spoken to Fiona's father, David, at the garage, and he had arranged for the car to be picked up and repaired. Michael jokingly reminded him of his comment about the reliability of Toyotas, but, as David said, at least it was still under warranty. Fortunately Michael was not requiring the car for a few days, and Fiona had her own, so there was no real problem. The shop was becoming busier by the day, and Fiona was being called on to help out on her non-working days, so she did not have much time to pursue the family history project. She was still waiting for the Downing/Roberts marriage certificate, and Michael had promised to find her some more photographs for the girls' folders. Although Fiona had said to Grace and Victoria that she was preparing a surprise for them for Christmas, it was looking ever more likely that this present would have to wait until their birthday at the beginning of March.

Sam Wainwright had told Michael the last time they spoke that he thought he would be back in Hopley before Christmas, and Michael was still worried at what Sam might say, although so far he had been fairly vague. Neither Fiona nor Paula told Michael about the telephone call, and when Sam did not return they were relieved, but puzzled. As he had died in a hotel room in Andover, about 45 miles away, this had not come to their attention.

Towards the end of November Fiona received the envelope she had been eagerly anticipating and dreading at the same time. Knowing what it was she kept the envelope away from Michael, and opened it in the kitchen while he was busy in the shop. She took a knife from the block on the work surface and sliced the envelope open. She gingerly took out the contents, the white covering letter falling to the floor as she unfolded the certificate. There it was – Michael Downing, bachelor, library assistant, age 34, father James Downing, postman, marrying Deborah Roberts, spinster, local government officer, age 31, father Frank Roberts, clerk, deceased, at St John's Church Emberton on 2 June 1987. She also noticed that Michael and Deborah were living together at 14 Clayton Road in Emberton. The address sounded familiar, but she could not recall why.

Fiona shook as she read the details. Her worst fears had been realised. She dropped the knife to the floor, where it landed with a clatter. Grabbing a chair she pulled it across the room and sat down, unable to quite believe what she had just read. She looked at the green piece of paper again. There was no mistake, it was the same man. She was staring at the certificate without really seeing it. Trying to gather her thoughts together she took a piece of scrap paper out of one of the kitchen drawers and started writing.

'Dear Michael,

I have just received this in the post ...'

She stopped and thought, then screwed up the paper. No, what was the point. She needed to find out more before talking to him. She needed to find out who this Deborah was? Why they got married? What happened to her? Where did Louise fit in this story? Was she, Fiona, really married at all? This marriage certificate had thrown up so many questions that she did not want to leave unanswered. One thing was certain; there was no way now that the twins' folders would be ready for Christmas.

Recovering her composure she decided upon her plan. First of all she would try to trace the details of both Deborah and Louise. Birth certificates could be ordered easily, and that would give a starting point. Information from those would give place and date of birth, together with parents. She could then trace any other marriages or deaths during the intervening years.

She would also try to contact Sam Wainwright. She could find Harpers Seeds telephone number via the Internet, and arrange to meet him to find out what he had to say, or if it was just as Paula had said, a fishing trip. Once she had received these pieces of information she would consider how best to tackle Michael on the subject. They had been married fourteen years, with no real problems, so she did not anticipate difficulties while she waited. Indeed with the rapid onset of Christmas there was not a great deal she could do.

With the information given on the marriage certificates of both Deborah and Louise she was easily able to trace their births, and so she ordered their birth certificates to see what they would reveal. She had already looked for Deborah's death unsuccessfully, but she continued to search after she and Michael were married, but again without success. She knew when Louise had died, but she sent for the death certificate to ensure she had the full facts in front of her. She rang Paula and told her briefly of the confirmation of the marriage, telling her also what she planned to do next. Paula expressed no surprise at this news, and she agreed with Fiona that her proposed course of action was the best one to pursue. They also agreed to get together after Christmas to discuss the situation.

Grace and Victoria were nearing the end of their first term at university. It had been a very successful start, they had enjoyed living away from home and the freedom that gave, and they had done well in their initial pieces of work. Having said that, they were looking forward to coming home for Christmas, and for their part Michael and Fiona were looking forward to their return also.

In December Michael worked six days a week, so it was on the Sunday before Christmas that he drove up to Birmingham to collect his daughters. The car had been repaired, although Michael was slightly nervous of taking it on a longish journey, but David had assured him it would not happen again. Despite that Michael knew he would be happy to be home.

Fiona had put all the family tree investigation onto one side now, and she decided she would not look at it again until the girls had returned to university after Christmas. The week prior to Christmas was always very busy, with everyone lending a hand. It was fun and a great family occasion that they all enjoyed. Christmas Eve closure arrived and they all collapsed into the nearest chairs. There were still the usual Christmas jobs to be done, but during the week the girls had been home they had cheerfully helped with decorating, baking, present buying and wrapping and all those little tasks that have to be done to make Christmas a joy. The lights in the town were particularly good this year, and all the shops seemed to have made a special effort to match them, with the result that the town was lit up as never before.

As they prepared to walk down the road to the church to attend the midnight service, Fiona felt a warmth as she was surrounded by her family that reminded her of when the twins were small, and they excitedly looked forward to Santa's visit. She had almost managed to forget the problems which her family tree tracing had brought, but as she saw a van drive along the road with emblazoned along the side, she realised that those problems were still very real. However she was determined not to let them spoil her Christmas, and as she walked into church and took her pew she fixed her mind on what she knew would be the choir's magnificent rendering of the descant.

Contrary to her expectations Fiona enjoyed Christmas. She always had enjoyed this time of year, but this year she had been somewhat apprehensive, owing to the unexpected findings of her investigations. Michael had provided her with some more photographs of him and Louise when the twins were little, and Fiona had done folders for Grace and Victoria as she had planned, but not with the amount of detail she had hoped for. She told them that there would be more to come.

After lunch on Christmas Day the girls had retreated to their bedrooms, and Michael was snoozing gently in his chair in the living room. Fiona looked across at him and remembered the good times they had had together. She was having difficulty reconciling this peaceful, placid man with the picture which was gradually emerging of a one with a mysterious past. He was still a good-looking man, she thought, and she could see how, in the past, he might have had many admirers, indeed she had been one. The charm that he exuded in his work, coupled with his good looks might also have made him vain, and she wondered if this had been a problem. Louise had been an attractive woman, tall, fair with a slim but shapely figure. She could see how they would have been drawn to each other. Fiona had known Louise through the shop, of course, and Michael had told her early on in their marriage, when he spoke of Louise more often, that she (Louise) had had a long-term relationship with an older man, with whom she had lived for six years, before meeting and then marrying Michael. He had recently admitted that Louise had been pregnant before they married, and that she had been anxious for them to be married before the birth of the twins, because she would be embarrassed to be shown on the birth certificate as unmarried. Somehow these facts, living with an older man for six years, being pregnant with Michael's children before marriage, and embarrassment at that fact being made public did not add up. It was another puzzle that Fiona felt she needed to find an answer to.

She was very content with the life that she and Michael had built together, and as she sat there watching him she wondered if it might have been better if she had not started to delve into his history. She was confident that Michael had been faithful to her during their marriage and she had been the same. Now the twins were away at university they had more time together to enjoy each other's company. Michael was very attentive and sensitive to her needs, and she liked that. He would bring her unusual presents, nothing expensive, but things she would never think of buying herself, and was always complimentary about her appearance. She felt very fortunate in having a husband who behaved like this, and knew from conversations with other women of a similar age that often their husbands did not match up to Michael's standard. Why, then, was she putting all this in jeopardy by carrying on with her project? The only answer she could come up with was that, in the words of Magnus Magnusson, she had started, so she would finish.

She walked out in to the kitchen and put the kettle on for a cup of tea. As the kettle boiled she cast her mind back to her conversation with Paula, and what she had said Sam Wainwright had said. If Michael was such a paragon, what was all this about Deborah Roberts? Why was it all such a secret? She made the tea and put out the cups and saucers. She called to Grace and Victoria and they came downstairs.

'Come on Dad, wake up. Are we going to play a game?'

Michael stirred in his chair. The family had

always been game players from the days when the girls were very young. Now they were ever on the lookout for new board games, and especially at Christmas they hoped to be able to find something different, which they usually did. This year they had found a new history-based game and a new word-based game, so both Grace and Victoria were catered for. Fiona brought through the tea, and Victoria set out the game. The rest of the day passed in uneventful family fun with Grace winning twice and Victoria once. Michael said jokingly that he was not going to play any more if they did not let him win occasionally.

The following day the whole family had been invited over to Peter and Paula Hamilton's house for lunch. When they arrived Peter met them at the door, looking downcast.

'What is it, Peter?' Michael asked.

'It's Danny,' he replied. 'You remember he was due to go to Afghanistan at some time.'

'Yes'

'Well, it's happened. He's been at home over

Christmas, but he had a call this morning telling him to report back to his barracks in Aldershot tomorrow, and they are flying out to Afghanistan at the weekend. Paula's taken it hard, although we knew it was coming. Just didn't know when. He's quite excited about it, which hasn't helped Paula. Joseph and Jane are ok but I suppose it's different for them.'

Michael and Fiona went in to the living room, which was neatly furnished with modern stylish armchairs and small tables. A plasma television hung on the wall at the far end of the room, with a stack of DVDs alongside a DVD player and satellite TV box. The room looked out on to a back garden which was equally neat, with box hedges, trimmed lawns and variegated bushes creating a severe and almost unwelcoming vista. Fiona went through into the kitchen where Paula was preparing a cold buffet for lunch. The kitchen was again neat and tidy, with everything in its place. Fiona put her arms around Paula, who was having difficulty holding back the tears.

'It's stupid, I know,' she said. 'But I hoped he

wouldn't really have to go. He's looking forward to it, which makes it worse somehow.'

She snuffled back her tears.

'How long is the tour?' Fiona asked.

'Three months initially.'

'Should be home in April then,' Fiona said brightly.

'Yes, hopefully.'

'Let me help you put these things out' Fiona said, as she picked up some plates and glasses. 'Let's enjoy today.'

Paula was thankful for her friend's attentions. It would make it easier to bear. As she walked through she heard Michael and Peter exchanging views on trading conditions in the town. Peter worked in a local high street Bank. Grace and Victoria were chatting to Jane, no doubt telling her about their first term, and probably expressing concern about Jane's unfortunate experience with Tom. All seemed perfectly normal and they tried to put away thoughts of the future as they spent a pleasant afternoon together, but there were dark clouds on the horizon, however much they all tried to ignore their own particular cloud.

During the afternoon Fiona managed to have a few words with Paula on her own.

'I can't go into it now, but I have lots to talk to you about. I have some new information, and I intend to find out more from After they are all back at university we need to have a day together to go through it all. It is becoming more and more problematic, but we haven't got time now.'

'You sound very worried,' Paula said.

'I suppose I am really, but maybe just puzzled. I can't work it all out. There are so many different strands to it all. And some of the facts just don't fit together, and don't fit with what I already know, or thought I knew.'

'We'll have a day at it,' said Paula. 'Would it be easier for you to come here, then we will be out of the way of any prying eyes, just in case.'

'Thanks, yes, I think that would be better. Michael is taking Victoria and Grace back on Monday 5 January. When do yours go back?'

'Joseph on Sunday 4 and Jane is going on the train on that Monday, the same as yours. What about the Tuesday that week? Or the Friday?'

'I think the Tuesday would suit me better, but Michael can be busy in the shop on Tuesdays and he likes me to be on hand, so maybe we'll go for the Friday.'

'Friday 9 then, it's a date. Come nice and early so we have plenty of time, then maybe we can go out for lunch somewhere.'

Fiona drove home in silence. Michael was also quiet but the girls chattered in the back of the car. They had said their goodbyes to Danny, and left in time for Paula and the family to spend the evening with him before his departure early the following morning.

'Paula isn't coping very well with Danny's posting,' said Fiona, once they were back home. 'To see your little boy going off to somewhere so dangerous must be very difficult. I don't know if I would be able to cope either.'

'No,' agreed Michael, 'it's difficult for any of us not in that situation to be able to understand what it must be like. Let's just hope that he comes through it ok. How was Jane after her ordeal? Has she got over it yet?'

'I think so. It has taken her longer than she thought it might. I suppose it's the loss of trust. You end up not being able to trust anyone. Bit like a husband or wife having an affair, I suppose.'

Michael looked at Fiona, and felt uncomfortable inside, although he tried not to show it.

'Yes. It must be,' he said. This subject was feeling a little too close to home for Michael's liking as he sought a change of subject. He put the television on to distract attention, which, fortunately, he thought, worked.

Michael closed the shop between Christmas and New Year as he thought he deserved a bit of time off. The family were, therefore, able to spend time together which was difficult at other times of year. Michael's parents had died many years before, and he had no contact with his brother. The only close family he had were Fiona, Grace and Victoria. Fiona's parents were still alive and Michael and the family spent New Year's Eve and New Year's Day with them. David and Megan Lewis did not have any grandchildren in Britain, although their son, Thomas, who had emigrated to Canada in 2001, now had three children, all boys, one of whom had been born since their move. Grace and Victoria were treated as grandchildren by the Lewises and they were always keen to catch up with whatever the girls had been doing.

The twins were nearly nineteen years old, and while they wanted to see their family, their time away had given them a feel for independence that they had not had before. This, in itself, was no problem, but

Fiona and Michael did notice that they became excited as the time approached for them to return to university,. Fiona had also noticed how they were starting to do separate things, and realised that their university time was very often spent apart.

When the time came for Michael to take them back to Birmingham Fiona took the opportunity to go with Michael, enabling her to see for the first time where the girls were living. soon met up with other students, and both Fiona and Michael felt surplus to requirements. They made a prompt getaway and as they were travelling back down the motorway Fiona decided it was time to try to find out a bit more about Michael's previous life.

'I think the girls liked their folders,' she started.

'Yes,' Michael replied, 'I'm sure they did.'

'Trouble is, I didn't know a great deal about Louise to put in them. Tell me more.'

Michael thought for a moment.

'I thought I had told you everything' he said.

'I want to feel that I've put everything I can

into the folders,' replied Fiona.

'Right,' said Michael, 'I'll start from the beginning. Louise and I worked in the same library in Emberton. She was born in London in 1960 and her parents were both teachers. They moved to Emberton when her father started a new job as head of English at Emberton High School. She was a clever girl and when she came to work at the library it was to train to become a qualified librarian. She was a very attractive woman, and her enjoyment of her social life got in the way of her studies. So she gave them up and continued to work as a library assistant. She had lived in Emberton with an older man, a Colin Fredrikson, for some years, six, I think, but that had faded. When I first met her she was living in her own house in Emberton. A couple of years after we met she got pregnant. It wasn't planned but we were both pleased. We married shortly after coming here. Like I said to you before Christmas when we were talking about the girls' birth certificates, we had wanted to marry before the birth, but events took over.'

I have heard this all before, apart from the bits

about her parents and school, thought Fiona.

Where is Deborah fitting in to all this? She decided that as Michael was driving it was not the best time to enquire about such things, but said;

'Yes, I know all that, apart from that about her parents, so I can add that in. I wondered if there was anything else.'

'There really isn't anything else to tell. You know that she was killed in a car accident and that's all there is.'

Fiona was still not sure about this explanation. It was almost too pat, too practised, but she had nothing else to help her at present. She did have the certificate information she had received just before Christmas, which she was going to talk to Paula about on Friday, but she wasn't sure that that was very helpful. Maybe Paula would have some better ideas.

She let the subject drop as they neared home. Michael's thoughts were on the business going into the New Year, and what improvements he could make to keep the shop profitable. He was constantly looking at new concepts and new ideas to combat the ever-present and growing threat from the big multiples, the Internet and now e-books. Bookselling was not a way to a fortune, but he was determined to stay profitable and earn a reasonable income.

Fiona was also thinking of the future, but in a different way. How was she going to reconcile all these disparate pieces of information she had gathered about Michael and his background. She was looking forward to Friday and her chat with Paula, and thought that when they arrived home she would carefully sort her thoughts into order, writing a summary of what might have happened. That way she would highlight the gaps and inconsistencies, which she could then address.

Michael was busy on the Tuesday, looking at which books publishers had held back from their Christmas lists, probably because they thought they were not strong enough to compete in that market. There was the usual crop of second-strand, if not second-rate, novels, a few biographies of lesser celebrities. But the main push was focussed on travel, holidays, maps and guides. He met with a couple of reps who expressed their concern over their own jobs, as more and more publishers were concentrating their efforts on either selling direct to the public, or to big wholesalers. Michael liked the interaction with the reps as he felt it gave him a more direct contact, but he appreciated that his relatively small orders would be hard to justify.

Fiona spent the day at home; she would be working Wednesday and Thursday and she wanted to be prepared for her day with Paula on Friday. She pulled out all the certificates she had bought and started to write her summary. As she did so Michael called through to her from the shop. As she walked through from the stockroom she saw him there, as usual, charming the customers and smiling sweetly at the attractive young rep that was waiting to see him. How could someone be so self-assured and confident if they had a shady background? Or maybe that was how people like that were able to get away with it. It seemed inconceivable to Fiona that there was not a sensible explanation to these family history problems, or perhaps she just did not wish to think the worst.

These thoughts swirled around her head as she took over from Michael in serving the customers.

Since starting on her family tree project back in September, Fiona had chatted to one or two customers who were doing the same thing. One of these was Mary Cole, a woman in her early sixties who called in to the shop regularly and liked to keep Fiona updated with her own discoveries. This morning she was very excited.

'Hello Fiona, glad you're here. I must tell you what I've found.'

Fiona looked around and saw that Michael had finished serving his customer.

'Are you ok, Michael,' she said, 'Mary has something to tell me.'

'Yes, you carry on, I'll be fine.'

Fiona took Mrs Cole through the back of the shop, and sat her down in the kitchen.

'I thought we would be more comfortable out

here. Now, what is it you have to tell me? You sound very excited.'

'I am,' replied Mary. 'Let me tell you from the beginning. I've been tracing my family for a number of years, as you know, but there has always been one strand of the story which has eluded me. It concerned my great-grandmother, my father's granny. I knew her name, but I have never been able to find anything out about her husband, or details of their son's, my granddad's, birth. Her name was Elizabeth, and she was born in 1870, that much I did know. I also knew that my granddad died in the First World War, leaving my granny with a little baby, my Dad. Granny subsequently remarried, and I don't think she ever knew anything about her first husband's birth. I suppose it was before the days of birthday cards, and it wasn't that important.'

'When I started to try to find granddad's birth I had very little to go on; a family story suggested his parents had been in Australia at some time, but I was unable to make any headway there. Then a distant relative said that she thought that someone in the family had been to South America, Argentina possibly. Granddad had a sister, born in this country around the turn of the century, and I ordered her birth certificate, which gave Alfred as her father. Unfortunately she died a few days after birth, so there are no descendants from her. I found this Alfred on a census, married with three children, living in Birmingham, but then he disappeared, leaving the wife and children, never to come back. Both Elizabeth and Alfred are missing from the same censuses and from that I assumed they were together somewhere. Then, by chance, when surfing the net for family history contacts in South America, I found a website that listed baptisms of children at British churches in Buenos Aires. I was amazed to find my granddad's baptism listed there. I was so excited. I then contacted a researcher in

Argentina who obtained the birth certificate, and she sent it to me. It gave all the details I needed, confirming the parentage and birth date, and giving me my granddad's grandparents as well. Everything slotted in to place. I even found Elizabeth and Granddad coming back to England on a boat when he was only two years old. Alfred seems to have vanished though, I have lost him completely. It seems as if Elizabeth eloped with this man when she was about twenty and he was twenty years older than her, married and with three children. I only know of the two children, but I would not be surprised if there were more in Argentina, but I have not been able to trace any. Then either she left him, or more likely, he left her as he had done with his wife. I don't think they ever married. What a scandal!'

Mary was almost breathless from the telling of this story, which Fiona thought sounded a little far-fetched.

'I know it sounds unlikely, but I've seen the

documents that prove it all.' she said. 'You can never tell what people can get up to. All those years ago as well. Travelling across the world like that. Of course, after Granddad died in the First World War and Granny remarried it was never mentioned again. Too disgraceful.'

Fiona listened carefully. Clearly Mary had done her research and was satisfied that this story was true. It was possible, if unlikely, but then, Fiona thought, people do the most unlikely things. It was so easy to put one's own view of the world on to someone else's actions and judge them accordingly. Whether it was something that happened twenty years ago or one hundred and twenty years ago, there would have been reasons and motivations behind particular actions that are difficult to understand today. Fiona was still thinking of Louise and Michael, and wondering about what really went on. Mary's tale of elopement, adultery and foreign adventures sounded so modern in many ways, but it all happened well over one hundred years ago. Maybe human nature does not change that much, maybe she should be looking at her own family history revelations with a slightly more jaundiced eye.

Fiona thanked Mary for telling her her story, and complimented her for her perseverance.

'Well done! It all sounds very complicated. What a find or series of finds, I should say. I don't think I have skeletons in any foreign cupboards, but you never know. But I shall bear in mind what you have said about family stories; they aren't always accurate, are they?'

'It's always nice to talk to you, Fiona,' said Mary, 'You're such a good listener. Thanks very much.'

Mary stood up and walked back through the stockroom into the shop.

'Goodbye, Fiona. Bye, Michael'

Mary left, and leaving Michael in the shop Fiona returned to the flat. She finished writing up her summary and put it together with the certificates on one side to take on Friday. There was one other enquiry she needed to make, and she closed the doors between the flat and shop quietly, as she didn't wish Michael to hear her making this telephone call. She had heard nothing from Sam Wainwright since well before Christmas, and she knew that Michael had not seen him either. This puzzled her as he had seemed very keen on talking to Michael again. She logged on to the Internet and keyed Harpers Seeds into the search engine. There it was – contact details for different parts of the Company; telephone, email and address. Sales, that's who she needed, she decided. Picking up the telephone she punched in the numbers.

'Good Morning, Harpers Seeds, Sales, Evie speaking, how can I help you?'

'Hello, can I speak to Sam Wainwright please?' Fiona said.

There was a noticeable pause at the other end.

'I'm sorry, what did you say?'

'Can I speak to Sam Wainwright please; he

does work for you, doesn't he?'

'Yes, sorry, I was a bit taken aback, that's all. Sam Wainwright died before Christmas. Can someone else help you?'

'No, it was Mr Wainwright I wanted to speak to. What happened?'

'He had a heart attack while he was out one day. In Andover, I think.'

Fiona was surprised, if not shocked, and either relieved or disappointed, she found it difficult to decide immediately.

'I'm very sorry to hear that. Did he have any family?'

'I can't tell you that, even if I knew,' said Evie. 'It was a shock to everyone in the company. We are a small family-run company and everyone knows everyone, so you can imagine how we all felt.'

Fiona gave her condolences, made her excuses and rang off. How could she tell Michael? She could not say she had phoned up and asked to speak to him. Better to say nothing, she thought, but it was something to add to her notes for Friday. Sam

Wainwright had been a potential troublemaker Fiona thought, but he had mentioned the name of Deborah, which she had subsequently turned up. She wondered what he really knew and how much he was guessing. Did he know enough to blackmail Michael? But what was there to blackmail Michael about? He had certainly known Michael in his Emberton days and there was something about him which had made Michael nervous. She remembered what she had thought when that woman's body had been found. I know about his first marriage to Deborah, although he probably doesn't realise I know, but that can't be all he was worried about, she reasoned. What else was there from back then that Michael was so concerned about, and that had distressed him so much? But since Christmas he had lost that edginess which had crept into his behaviour. Perhaps he had just forgotten about Sam, or maybe he knew that he was dead and no longer a problem. She shivered at that thought and put it away immediately, but she could not deny that it had crossed her mind. Then she remembered that Sam had died of a heart attack.

Fiona tried to tell herself that she was being silly, and that her husband was a good man, faithful and honest. Why, then, did she keep having these thoughts about him, these imaginings of wicked deeds from years ago? Then she remembered Mary Cole and her tale of past misdemeanours in her family.

Michael was calling again and she went back into the shop. She would concentrate for the rest of the day on the present and her work, and forget the past. However Friday could not come quickly enough. She needed Paula's level head to sort out these conflicting stories, and set her mind at rest. She buried herself in her work, and that night, in bed, when Michael put his arms around her and drew her to him, she forgot all her worries.

It was a cold, raw morning as Fiona drew up in the car outside Paula's house. She wrapped her coat around her as she stepped out of the warmth of the car into the biting wind. Picking up her folder she hurried up the path to the front door. Paula had seen her coming and opened the door quickly.

'Come in, quick,' she said. 'I've got the heating full on; it's so cold out there.'

Fiona took her coat off and went in. Paula put the kettle on for tea for Fiona and went to make her coffee.

'I thought it would be better in the dining room,' she said, 'more space.'

Fiona walked through and began to take out a sheaf of papers, which she spread out over the dining room table.

'How's Danny?' Fiona asked, remembering how upset Paula had been at his departure.

'Fine, so far,' replied Paula, 'we had an email from him the other day to say they had arrived safely and were getting used to the climate and surroundings. I'm still worried about him, but I shouldn't be.'

'Why not? You're his mum. If you can't be worried about him, who can?'

'What about yours? All settled back in?'

'Yes, no problems there, thank goodness.'

Paula went back into the kitchen as she heard the kettle boil. She made the tea and brought through a tray with biscuits, together with her coffee.

'Now, tell me what you have been finding out.'

'There's a lot to tell.' said Fiona. 'But first of all let me tell you about George Cartwright.'

'Who's he?'

'My granny's twin brother, the one who died a few months after birth.'

'Oh yes, I remember now.'

'Now I knew a lot of this already, but I wanted a full picture. You remember we were looking at times of birth? Well, he was born at 2.50pm, twenty minutes before my granny, so he was the older twin. He died aged four months, hydrocephalus and convulsions it said on the death certificate.'

'How sad. In some ways all of this is sad, isn't it?' said Paula.

'Yes, I know what you mean. It's all sex and death; which brings me neatly to Michael and Deborah. I told you about the marriage between Michael and Deborah Roberts, didn't I? Well, after that came, I decided to build up a complete picture of what has happened. You know, if it hadn't been for that idea about the folders for the girls, and that mysterious time on my grandmother's birth certificate I wouldn't be doing any of this. But now I can't let it go. I must find out.'

'So, to start at the beginning. I searched online for the dates when Michael, Deborah and Louise were born, and then I sent for their birth certificates. Here they are.'

She handed the papers across to Paula, who

looked at them with interest.

Fiona continued:

'Michael Downing, born 12 July 1952, at 37 Burnside Avenue, Emberton, father, James Downing, postman, mother, Anne Downing, formerly Sutherland.'

'Deborah Roberts, born 3 June 1955, at 14 Clayton Road, Emberton, father, Frank Roberts, clerk, mother, Alice Roberts, formerly Bingham.'

'Louise Baxter, born 17 September 1960, at 23, West Place, Streatham, father Edward Baxter, schoolmaster, mother, Catherine Baxter, formerly King.'

'These seem fairly straightforward,' Paula said, 'what next?'

'Here's the marriage certificate between Deborah and Michael. You will see that the information fits perfectly. There is no doubt that they are the same people.'

Paula stared at the birth certificates and the marriage certificate as if looking at them would make the information change.

'I don't understand it,' she said, at last.

'No, neither do I,' agreed Fiona. 'By the way, you remember that Sam Wainwright chap, the seed rep you spoke to on the phone? Well, he's dead.'

'What?'

'Yes, I rang Harpers Seeds the other day because I wanted to meet him. He had mentioned a Deborah, and it looks as though there was some truth in what he was saying, but I wanted to find out what exactly he knew. Anyway I'm not going to find out now, at least from him. He had a heart attack, apparently. The girl on reception didn't tell me much, but it seems as if he died in a hotel room whilst he was on one of his trips.'

'Michael always looked awkward when he was around or when he was mentioned,' Fiona continued. 'I'm not sure what it was but it was as if he had some hold over him.'

'What sort of hold?'

'I've no idea, except that I am guessing it had something to do with this Deborah.'

'He said that he'd met Deborah at a social function at the athletics club.' Paula reminded Fiona. 'He didn't seem to know much more than that. What else have you got?'

'I looked for Deborah's death, either as Deborah Roberts or Deborah Downing, but I couldn't find anything. Just look at Michael's marriage to Louise.'

Fiona handed the Downing/Baxter certificate to Paula. Michael describes himself as a bachelor. Why would he do that? If Deborah had died he would be a widower, or if they'd divorced, he would have been a divorcee. He couldn't be a bachelor under any circumstances.'

'Perhaps,' said Paula, 'Deborah had left him and he was too ashamed to admit it, so said he was a bachelor.'

'But that would make him a bigamist,' protested Fiona, 'both with Louise and with me.'

'Not necessarily. He might have been divorced, but if she'd left him for another man he might have felt he couldn't admit it, so he just pretended.'

'Possibly.'

'How can we find that out?' Paula asked 'Is there a list of divorces?'

'Hmm. Not sure.'

Fiona pondered this idea.

'If that were the case, what hold would Sam Wainwright have over Michael? What crime would Michael have committed? Apart from being embarrassed that his wife has left him, and that's no crime. And if he were divorced then it would only affect me and I wouldn't care, and I wouldn't think these days that anyone else would either.'

Fiona remembered the story that her customer Mary Cole had told her about her great-grandmother and her eloping with a married man. Maybe Deborah left Michael for someone else, went abroad, and he has not heard of her since. He then met Louise, fell in love, she got pregnant and they wanted to marry. They couldn't marry in Emberton because everyone knew he was already married, so after he and Louise moved to Hopley they married and Michael pretended to be a bachelor, and no one was any the wiser. Unfortunately by then Louise has had the twins, so Michael put Louise down as his wife to complete the, fairly minor, deception.

Having thought this through Fiona explained her theory to Paula, and they both thought it was the most likely explanation.

'Yes, I think you could be right, Michael and Deborah don't have to be divorced.' said Paula. 'Of course, Deborah could have died after she left him. In that case you might be married to him legitimately.'

'But if she is not dead and they were not divorced, then I am not married to Michael and he has committed bigamy twice. What is the sentence for bigamy? Can you go to prison?'

'That's a very gloomy thought,' said Paula,

'who knows anyway, even if it is true? Unless there is another Sam Wainwright waiting in the wings somewhere. But you've been living here for fourteen years and nothing has come up so far. Why should it now?'

'Come on, let's cheer up and go and have some lunch. Where do you fancy? We could go to the if you like, or try the

A taste of the Mediterranean on a nasty day like today sounds very attractive. Let's go to the replied Fiona, remembering the pub's reputation.

They wrapped themselves in layers of clothing and walked out to Fiona's car, parked in the road. As they got in Fiona said;

'There's something I think we're missing. I have this feeling that there's something staring us in the face that we've missed which will unlock this mystery, and I think the answer is on those certificates.'

'Come on, stop fretting. Let's go and have some lunch. Take your mind off it.'

They drove back across town and parked in the car park behind the pub. Fiona was still deep in thought.

'Fi, stop it! We are going to have some lunch and you are going to think of other things for an hour. We'll then go back home and have another look for this mystery.'

'Sorry, Paula. You're right. Let's have a look at the menu.'

The women were spoiled for choice but eventually Paula chose the spinach and mushroom frittata, while Fiona had the Mediterranean courgette pie. As she was driving Fiona had a fruit juice but Paula had a glass of white Italian wine. The conversation moved away from families and marriages as the two women savoured the food they had not had to cook.

'Excellent,' said Fiona, 'everyone always says how good it is, but I haven't been for ages. Our anniversary last year was the last time, I think.'

'Yes, it was; excellent, I mean. Let's ask for the bill.'

The young waiter brought across the bill, with a smile that was not quite genuine. However, it became more genuine when he saw how generous these two customers had been with their tip.

The day was still cold as they returned to the car. The lunch had given a hint of sunshine and warmth, but that was a long way off in reality. Driving back to Paula's house Fiona was once again lost in the past. She was sure that there was a clue to this mystery in those certificates but she could not identify it. The dark clouds carrying the rain and sleet which was starting to fall reflected how she felt, and she felt as helpless trying to stop the rain as she did trying to unlock this conundrum. She and Paula rushed indoors, back to the warmth and comfort of Paula's dining room. The various certificates, spread out on the table, seemed to look at the two women, challenging them to decipher them, and solve the problem. Fiona took out the copies of the birth certificates of the twins, and put them on the table alongside the others.   She now had the complete set, ranging from all the births, the two marriages, three if she included her own, Louise's death certificate, and Grace and Victoria birth certificates.   She looked and looked at these pieces of paper, reading them all closely.   Suddenly her eyes lit up.

'Paula, look!'

'What? What have you found?' asked Paula.

'Look at the twins' birth place, and then look at Deborah's address on her marriage certificate.'

'Oh, my goodness!' Paula exclaimed, '14, Clayton Road, Emberton. It's the same! That seems to add to your problems, not solve them, doesn't it?'

'I'm not really sure.'

'You have got both Louise's and Deborah's birth certificates, so we know they are not the same person.'

'We also know Louise died in that car accident. Michael identified her. He told me once how dreadful it was. Her face was badly cut from where the windscreen had been pushed in on to her. They didn't let him see the rest of the body. He thinks it was because she was so badly damaged,' added Fiona.

'Whatever has gone on Michael must have been in on it. Is it possible that Michael identified the car crash victim as Louise when it was Deborah? Although I can't see why he would do that. And even if he had done, where is Louise? We need to know why the girls were born at Deborah's house. Or did Michael lie about that as well?'

'So if Louise really was Louise Baxter, and the mother of Grace and Victoria, where is Deborah? We are back where we were before lunch. Left him, divorced or dead.'

'This is making my head spin,' said Paula. 'I shall put the kettle on and sit and think about it.'

She went into the kitchen, leaving Fiona in the dining room, wondering. A few moments later Paula came through carrying a tray with steaming cups of tea and a plate of tempting biscuits.

'What was it that Sam Wainwright had said? Dark haired and curvy. That was how he described the Deborah he had come across. Louise was tall, fair and slim and Michael said shapely, but I don't think he meant curvy in the sense that Sam did. There is no way that Deborah and Louise can be the same person. Indeed Sam said he had seen Louise in the library and he certainly did not say that it was Deborah whom he had seen there.'

'In that case, if Louise was definitely the car accident victim, which I think we have to accept, then we need to trace the whereabouts of Deborah.' said Fiona.

She didn't look too keen on this outcome of their discussions but it seemed the only option.

'After Deborah had left, for whatever reason, Michael and Louise must have lived at 14, Clayton Road, and Louise gave birth there. The girls were born in early March so Deborah must have left before then,' Fiona continued, 'maybe I will have to ask

Michael; at least that way we'll find the answer once and for all.'

'I think you'll have to,' said Paula. 'It's too complicated otherwise.'

Fiona flopped down into one of the easy chairs in the corner of the room.

'Thanks Paula. You've been a real friend over this, but I think we've come to a dead end now. I'll find a moment to raise it with Michael when he's had a good day, and find out what went on. It will probably only be in bits, though. I can't see him telling me everything all at once. He's had chances to do that in the past, in fact only the other day he said he'd told me everything, but that isn't right, is it?'

Fiona was disappointed that she had not been able to persuade Michael to tell her the whole truth, and that worried her slightly. The doubts about his life before Louise persisted, and she had been unable to dispel them. In fact, there seemed to be more questions every time she looked into it. The short day was drawing to its early close as Fiona gathered up her papers, ready to go home. The rain was now turning more defiantly to sleet, and the wind was colder than it had been all day. She put on her coat and wrapped her scarf around her neck for added warmth.

'We'll have another session soon,' Fiona said as she walked out to the car. 'Once I have spoken to Michael.'

She drove home through the rain and the sleet, her brain in a whirl. She needed more time to think about what to do next. Maybe she should speak to the girls, she thought, but then dismissed the thought just as quickly. It would only upset them.

She arrived home just as Michael was shutting up shop for the day.

'Enjoy your day?' he asked, 'How is life at the Hamiltons?'

'Yes, thanks. We had an excellent lunch at the as well. Funny waiter there, though.'

'Yes, I remember him from when I went there with Sam Wainwright.'

Fiona busied herself with household matters and no more mention was made of Sam, Paula or family history.

Christmas was receding fast and the cold, miserable days of January were well entrenched. Fiona had not yet spoken to Michael on the questions which had arisen out of her conversation with Paula; indeed she was wondering whether she would ever be able to broach the subject at all. There was clearly something in Michael's past, which she did not know, and which he was keen she did not discover. For the fourteen years of their marriage Michael had been a good, dutiful husband, and she realised that she was putting all that at risk with these investigations. However, having said that, she also knew that she could not let matters rest for the future. These facts would eat away at her until she found the answers, and not finding the answers might be as damaging to her future relationship with Michael as finding them. She was, therefore, determined to solve this mystery sooner or later.

The flat and the shop had different postal addresses, and while the postman was usually able to deliver the shop post to the shop and the home post to the flat, this did not always happen. So it was, one day in the middle of January, that a letter addressed to Michael Downing, care of the shop, was delivered to the flat. Fiona picked up the post and looked at the envelope. It was clearly a personal letter, not business, but with unfamiliar writing, and with an unreadable postmark. She took the letter through into the shop.

'Letter from an admirer, by the looks of it,' she teased, as she handed the letter to him. Michael looked at the envelope and was unable to recognise the writing. Intrigued, he took the letter opener off the desk and sliced the envelope open. Taking the contents out he unfolded the single piece of paper and started to read

it read:

Yours truly

Linda Downing

Michael went white as he dropped the letter on to the desk in front of him. Fiona picked it up and read it.

'Who is Linda Downing?' asked Fiona.

'She's my sister-in-law. Ian was three years younger than me. I haven't seen or heard from him or Linda for over twenty years. As you know, we didn't get on as children, then as we grew up our differences became more marked. I remember when we were little boys we played together and all seemed well, but then he went to the grammar school and that seemed to make him think he was better than me. He had different friends who looked down on me. They said I was thick because I went to the secondary modern school, and Ian went along with it. I think he ended up believing it. Then when our parents became ill and needed nursing care he refused to help out with the fees. They both had dementia before they died, just after the girls had been born as it happens. He had a good job but said his family came first; they had three boys, and he said he couldn't afford it. Of course at that time I had no children, and so Ian thought I was in a better position to help pay the fees. What with everything else it was just the last straw. I know Mum and Dad died a long time ago now, but it was never the right time to get back together, and now it's too late.'

Fiona put her arms around him.

'What shall we do about the funeral, then? Do you want to go?'

'I don't know. It's a Wednesday, isn't it? Wednesdays are difficult, you're at work. I suppose I should, but…'

His voice trailed off.

'What do you think? Should I go?'

'Paula could do the shop for you, if you want

to.'

'No, I don't think I can go. With all that has happened in the past, I don't think I could face it... and Linda especially.'

'It's really up to you. If you don't want to go, don't go. Are you going to write and say so, or would you like me to do that?'

'Yes, maybe. I am rather surprised Linda managed to find me here anyway. I wonder if she contacted the library in Emberton. They might have pointed her in my direction.'

Fiona was not surprised that Michael did not want to go to the funeral. He might be asked awkward questions by people he knew from a long time ago.

'Michael, are you sure you want me to write? I could say that you had an urgent appointment which you could not break.'

'Yes, do that, I really can't go.'

'If you are sure.'

This was another aspect of Michael's past of which she knew nothing. How much more was there? She wondered.

Michael picked up the letter and read it again. He wished that Ian had let him know when he was ill before, but he knew it was always so difficult to make that first step, on either side, and then it was too late.

'I never really liked Linda,' he said. 'I don't even know why really. She was very bossy and kept Ian in his place, maybe that was it. She might've changed over the years, who knows? Probably not, people don't, do they? I never could stand bossy women. Do this, do that, don't do this, don't do that.'

Fiona listened with interest. This was sounding very personal, but Fiona had never had the impression that Louise was like that, and she knew that she wasn't. The doorbell rang as customers came into the shop.

'I'll go and make you a cup of tea,' Fiona said.

Fiona went through into the kitchen and put the kettle on. As Michael was busy she rang Paula and told her of the letter and Michael's reaction. She also said she had an idea that she would go to the funeral without telling Michael, with the intention of finding out more about his background. She acknowledged that it seemed underhand, but felt that it was justified in the present circumstances. Paula was very supportive of her idea and asked Fiona to keep her fully informed. A few minutes later she took the tea through to Michael in the shop. As she did so she showed him a sealed envelope addressed to Linda.

'Here you are. Done it,' she said.

'Thanks, what did you say?' asked Michael, disappointed that Fiona had not shown him the letter.

'I explained why you couldn't come, saying that you had a long-standing appointment at the local hospital. I said it was for a minor operation which you couldn't cancel because it would have meant waiting a long time before a new appointment could be scheduled. I told her that I was your second wife because your first wife had been killed in a car crash. And, of course, I expressed my sorrow at her loss; and yours, of course.'

Fiona took the letter, put her coat on and walked out of the shop. Walking down to the post office she considered what Michael had said. Here was a part of his family which he had never spoken about before, and which he may never speak about again, and yet he clearly cared, or he would not have reacted as he did. No Christmas cards, no Birthday cards, no nothing, but some residual care, nonetheless. What else was there about her husband that she did not know?

She would be able to arrange time off from

work to attend a family funeral without too much difficulty, and Michael would think she was at work. The rain was being blown horizontally by a sharp, cold wind. She was not looking forward to standing at a graveside in this sort of weather, paying her respects to a man she never knew.

Fiona had not mentioned in the letter her intention to attend the funeral. She thought it better to turn up on the day, rather than give Linda the opportunity of replying to Michael expressing regret at his non-attendance, and saying how she was looking forward to meeting Fiona. It had been very straightforward getting time off work. Michael, of course, had no idea when Fiona left that morning that she was not going to Unity Insurance, but to his brother's funeral. She felt rather deceitful as she pulled away from the flat, but convinced herself she was doing what was necessary. She would deal with the ramifications of her visit at a later date, if, indeed, that was required.

It was an hour and a half's journey to Maddingfield, and as the funeral was at 12.30pm Fiona was able to arrive in plenty of time to have a bite to eat before the service. It was a crisp January day, snow having fallen for the first time that winter, but the roads were clear. On her arrival Fiona found the church in the centre of the village, and parking nearby went for a walk around and a peek inside the church. The church was mainly fourteenth-century, with a squat tower on the north-west corner of the building. There had been various additions over the years, including the almost standard Victorian restoration, but it was well-maintained, with polished brass work, shiny pews and clean carpets. The East window with its depiction of the resurrection looked magnificent, and the stained glass in the side aisle windows threw coloured shapes on to the floor of the nave, where the sun was shining. Modern hymn books and prayer books jostled with older Books of Common Prayer on the shelves inside the door, displaying a refreshing breadth of worship styles. Maddingfield appeared to be a wealthy village, with smart thatched cottages surrounding the church, as they had done for two hundred years and more. Well-kept gardens were visible from the road, along with garages for the Range Rovers, BMWs and Jaguars of the cottage occupants.

Despite their lack of contact over the years

Michael knew that Ian and Linda had lived in the village for many years, and so would have been well known locally. Fiona later discovered that Ian had worked as a manager on a local farm, and had become something of an expert in organic farming in recent years. Knowing how long Ian had lived in the village, Fiona expected that the church would be full with family and friends. After a pleasant snack at the local pub Fiona walked slowly towards the church. She slipped inside, and sat in one of the back pews. She knew no-one, and so she would have to guess who the family were from the way they conducted themselves, and where they sat. A few people drifted in after twelve o'clock, and Fiona was surprised that even by the start of the service, there were so few mourners, the church being only half-full by the time the funeral party arrived. Just before twelve thirty she heard the priest intone the words which have been gracing funerals for well over three hundred years

'I am the resurrection and the life, saith the Lord: he that believeth in me, though he were dead, yet shall he live: and whosoever liveth and believeth in me shall never die.'

The priest, a small man with greying hair, immaculately dressed in black cassock, white starched surplice and purple stole entered the Church followed by the coffin, borne on the shoulders of six men, three of whom looked remarkably like Michael, and whom she guessed must be Ian's sons. A well-built woman followed, wearing a large black hat, edged with a veil which fell across her face. A black coat and skirt, and black shoes completed the attire of the woman Fiona thought, correctly, was Linda. The cortege moved through the Church as the priest continued, with the coffin being placed on trestle supports at the head of the nave, and the bearers and Linda moving to the side to sit in the front pews. The service proceeded as normal, but with, unusually, four hymns interspersing the prayers. Towards the end of the service, during which there had been a short eulogy given by one of the sons, the priest invited the mourners to come out into the churchyard for the committal, and afterwards to join Linda and the family at home for refreshments. Fiona followed at a respectful distance as the priest led the coffin and mourners to the graveside. She was grateful that the weather was not that which she had feared, when she had first read the letter about Ian.

Not knowing Ian or the family, Fiona had just let the words of the service flow over her without any personal involvement in the proceedings, but she realised that whilst doing so she was transported by the words and cadences of the prayers and hymns. In this way she felt a closeness to Linda and her family that she might not have felt if she had known them better. As the priest returned to the Church, the other mourners started to walk out of the Churchyard towards a row of cars which were parked nearby. Fiona hesitated, not knowing where to go, when she was approached by Linda.

'Hello, I'm Linda. And you are...?'

'Hello, yes. Sorry, I didn't mean to gatecrash. I'm Fiona, Michael's wife. It only seemed right for one of us to come. Please accept my condolences. I didn't know Ian, of course. Sorry, that's obvious, isn't it?'

Fiona stifled an embarrassed laugh.

`Hello, Fiona, I'm so glad that you came, I was hoping you might,' said Linda, 'I do understand. It's awkward at things like this, when you don't know anybody. Anyway, thank you very much for coming. It's much appreciated. Where are you parked?'

Fiona indicated her Toyota Yaris parked a few yards away.

'Just there.'

'It's not very far, follow me.'

Linda stepped into the main limousine and the car pulled silently away. Fiona quickly got into her car and followed to the edge of the village, where there was a housing estate of newer properties, comparing unfavourably with the thatched cottages near the church. The limousine stopped outside number seven, an unprepossessing three-bedroomed semi-detached house, a copy of which could be found almost anywhere in the country. Linda emerged from the car, and was quickly followed by her three sons and two of their wives, who were in the second limousine. Fiona parked as near as she could to the house and walked, rather nervously, up to the front door. Before she was able to knock, the door opened and an attractive young man greeted her.

'Hello, I'm Jamie, and this is my wife, Sadie,' he introduced a young girl, whom Fiona did not think looked old enough to be married. On second thoughts Fiona just decided she must be getting old.

'You're Fiona, aren't you? Mum told me about you and Uncle Michael.'

'Yes, I am. I'm sorry to meet you in such sad circumstances.'

Fiona edged forwards into the living room

which was crowded with other guests. A small congregation in a Church is a lot of people in a small house.

'Hello again, Fiona,' greeted Linda, 'Let me get you a drink. What would you like? You're driving, aren't you? '

'Yes. Orange juice will be fine,' replied Fiona. 'Thanks.'

'I see you've already met Jamie and Sadie,' continued Linda, 'they only got married at Christmas. They wanted to do it before Ian died so that he could see all his children married.'

Linda pointed across the room to another brother.

'That's my eldest son and his wife, Matthew and Rachel, and that...' she said, turning round towards the front window of the room, and pointing to a young man with a drooping moustache and shoulder-length hair,

'... is my middle son, Jonathan. His appearance is a bit old fashioned but he is very up-to-date really. He works as an alternative energy consultant with BP. His wife, Cordelia, is a professional charity worker. Unfortunately she is in New York on business at the moment, and she couldn't get back in time for the funeral. She's a lovely girl though, and I know she would have come if it had been at all possible.'

Fiona marvelled at how calm and collected Linda was, introducing her family as if it were a summer party, not her husband's wake.

'Don't worry about me,' Linda said, 'I have been expecting this for a long time. When Ian was ill before we were all prepared, but he made a remarkable recovery. But we knew it was only a matter of time. Ian had prepared everything in advance, church service, wake and guests. He even tracked down Michael through the library where he used to work, and although he did not want to contact him, he left it to me to decide. To be truthful, my dear, I wanted to meet you once I had discovered that Michael had remarried. I am so sorry to hear about Deborah, though, dying in that awful accident. Did you know her?'

Fiona looked rather startled by what she had just said.

'Sorry, my dear,' said Linda, noticing Fiona's discomfort, 'it must have been dreadful for Michael. The last time we saw them she was pregnant, about five months, I think. What did she have? Must be grown up now. How time flies. Of course, we didn't see a lot of them.'

Fiona could not believe her ears. What did she mean? Deborah pregnant? How did this fit in with the other facts she had learned recently? She would have to say something.

'Yes, very sad. A girl. She's at university now.' Fiona was having to make this up as she went along. She answered the question as if it had been asked about one of the twins; it was all she felt she could do. She would then investigate more closely when she returned home.

Fortunately for Fiona, Linda drifted away to speak to some of the other guests, and she was able consider what Linda had just said. Fiona had gone to the funeral with the idea of finding out a little more about Michael and Deborah, but she had not expected this. She spoke briefly to one or two of the other guests; they were mainly Ian's work colleagues and neighbours. She got the impression that Ian was well-respected locally, but maybe not liked very much. Perhaps that is why the church was not as full as it might have been.

Time was moving on and she had a long journey home. She needed to be back in Hopley to appear to return from work at the right time, so she decided to make her excuses and leave. Finding her way back across the room to Linda she thanked her, and Linda thanked her in return. The two women agreed that they would keep in touch in the future, exchanging telephone numbers and email addresses, and said they wanted to try to mend the mistakes of the past. There were snow flurries as Fiona started her journey home, but fortunately they did not turn into anything substantial. As she drove Fiona could not stop thinking about what Linda had said; five months, so who was that?

Fiona arrived home just as if she had been to work. Michael was cooking a meal, which he did occasionally on her work days, and was sitting in front of the television watching cricket highlights from Australia, waiting for the cooker to announce that the meal was cooked.

'Hello,' he said 'Good day?'

Fiona had been planning what to say all the way home. It was becoming more and more difficult to deal with all the different pieces of information coming her way, especially as they nearly all reflected badly on Michael.

'Yes, nothing special. It was Ian's funeral today, I wonder how that went. OK I hope.'

'Linda was always very organised. Well, so was Ian, come to that. I expect it went like clockwork. A place for everything and everything, and everyone, knowing Linda, in its place.'

'Michael, that sounds very harsh. Were they that bad?'

Fiona was thinking back to her conversation with that pleasant, friendly woman she met at the funeral. Michael's description of her did not tally at all. But then, she thought, a lot of what I am learning about Michael and his past does not tally

'They were always very self-contained,'

Michael replied, 'Their house, their jobs, their children; that was what was important. They were never interested in anything anyone else was doing. So as far as Ian's funeral was concerned everyone was there for them, so that would have been fine from Linda's point of view.'

'So is that why you fell out?' enquired Fiona.

'In a way, I suppose. As I said it was about the fees for Mum and Dad. But it comes to the same thing. Nothing was allowed to get in the way of how they wanted to live their life. The fees for Mum and Dad were just a symptom of that.'

The cooker beeped its warning and Michael continued with his cooking duties.

'Come on,' he said, 'Forget about that now, let's eat.'

Fiona and Michael spent the rest of the evening in companionable silence. She did not want to talk too much about the day, because of what she had been told, but she was anxious to discuss this with Paula. She sat quietly completing the crossword while Michael continued watching the cricket. As they prepared for bed, Michael gave Fiona a desultory kiss, and she felt a coldness from him which she had not experienced before.

Deborah five months pregnant? She returned to her previous thoughts. Linda had not said when it was that she and Ian had last seen Michael, but he said it was twenty years. How did that fit with the twins and Louise? Perhaps Deborah died in childbirth with the child she was expecting then. It was strange that Michael had never mentioned Deborah, or that she had been expecting a child. Maybe he was so distressed by it all that he had put the whole thing out of his mind; so much so that he had described himself as a bachelor on his marriage to Louise. When Sam Wainwright had turned up Michael had been upset at the memories that he had resurrected, and that would have explained his odd behaviour.

She turned over and settled down to sleep, but

there was still a nagging doubt at the back of her mind.

Madeleine Porter sipped her morning coffee as she stood in the kitchen of the bungalow she shared with her brother Tim Lock. She was a petite woman with grey hair falling to her shoulders. She had never been able to afford expensive clothes, and she was most at home wearing jumpers or cardigans, with trousers or jeans and 'sensible' shoes. Looking at her it was difficult to imagine she had given birth to five children all of whom had left home some years ago and were now well-established in their own lives. Madeleine had been widowed two years ago when her husband, Richard, the vicar of a neighbouring parish, had died suddenly of a heart attack. There had been no warning, and Madeleine, left on her own at the relatively young age of fifty-seven, was having to adjust very quickly to life of a quite different sort. Richard and Madeleine had spent the whole of their married life living in various vicarages, and they never had enough money to buy a separate house for their retirement. As a result, when Richard died, although the Church was very good to her, and she was in receipt of a clergy widow's pension, she had to move out of the vicarage.   Madeleine's brother, Tim, had never married, and he lived on his own in a bungalow on the outskirts of Emberton. When his sister was widowed, it seemed only natural for her to come and live with him, especially as they had always got on so well together. Tim was pleased to have the company, and he always liked to see Madeleine's family as he had been over the years a very favoured uncle, and now great-uncle. For her part Madeleine found it very helpful having Tim around during the first weeks and months after Richard's death, and they had now settled into a comfortable, mutually beneficial lifestyle.

Madeleine was watching Tim cut the hedges and trim the trees in the back garden. He had read somewhere that you ought to do these jobs before the end of January, before the birds started nesting. He was taller than Madeleine, although he would never be described as tall, and was broad-shouldered and deep-chested. He had had very dark brown hair to match his dark eyes. The hair was greyer now, but the eyes were still an asset. He was dressed in his gardening clothes, but unlike his sister, he was equally comfortable in smarter attire. Tim had worked in the planning office for Emberton Borough Council, but when there had been a reorganisation of local government back in 1994 he had moved to the County Council, now more properly described as a Unitary Authority, but doing much the same job.

Madeleine waited for the whirring of the hedge-trimmer to stop, then opened the back door and called to her brother.

'Tim. Coffee's up.'

Tim looked round and grinned. His broad smile complemented his bright eyes in a way that Madeleine had always been able to see would be attractive to women, and Tim had not been shy in putting it, and them, to good use. There had been a wide variety of girlfriends over the years but only one who had become anywhere near permanent. He put the hedge-trimmer down carefully and walked up to the kitchen door,

'Can you switch off at the plug, please?' he asked.

He took off his gardening gloves and brushed the bits and pieces of hedge off his trousers as he walked into the kitchen.

'Thanks. Lovely,' he said as he picked up the steaming mug appreciatively.

'Any biscuits?'

Madeleine handed him the biscuit barrel containing his favourites. Since they had been living together they had come to a remarkably quick accord as to who bought what, and what type of things they bought. They knew each other's favourites and were pleased to accommodate each other. Tim was a keen gardener and spent as much of his spare time as possible outside cutting, pruning, sowing and reaping. Madeleine thought that he would have made an excellent smallholder in days gone by, and as he was now deskbound at work, he enjoyed the fresh air that gardening brought him. Madeleine was more of an indoor person. Having raised five children and having a husband who worked from home, although she could never quite work out whether he worked from home or they lived at his work, she preferred the quiet of a good book or a crossword puzzle in her free time. Now, of course, she had more free time than she had ever been used to, and she had bought herself a small computer on which she was learning new skills.

Like many others, she had been inspired to search her family tree by the television programmes which had sprung up recently. The new computer was proving a boon, and she was becoming very proficient, to such an extent that she had put an advertisement in the parish magazine to help others do the same. Sadly, for her, though, this venture had not proved to be a success, but she was pleased with the progress she was making with her own family. Tim was not particularly interested in her discoveries, although it was his family as well, but occasionally she shared information with him that she thought he might find interesting.

Madeleine sat down at the kitchen table alongside Tim. He was staring out of the window, engrossed in his thoughts about what to do next in the garden. Whether it was January or June, Tim knew there was a job which needed doing, and he liked the rhythm that this brought to the year and to his life. He had worked in planning for so long that it was now no more than a means of making enough money to live and fund his garden pleasures. Once he had enjoyed the challenge of the work, but it had now deteriorated into a box-ticking exercise, or so he thought. If he had the opportunity he would leave tomorrow, but he knew that was not possible.

'I had some interesting post this morning,' Madeleine said.

Tim guessed that this was family-history related, as this was how the conversation invariably started.

'Great-great grandfather George Mountford died in a mining accident in 1852. I got his death certificate this morning. I wondered about what happened and whether anyone else was hurt, so I looked the accident up on the Internet. It was terrible; there were fifty-three fatalities in this accident which was caused by poor safety or inadequate precautions being taken. There were reports in the local and national press at the time, but with little criticism of the employers. They mainly blamed the employees for not doing their jobs properly. The article on the internet said that these kinds of accidents were commonplace, and that as the newspaper owners were from the same or similar background to the mine owners, it was unlikely that the press would hold the mine owners to account.'

'It was 1852, remember, not 2012,' said Tim. 'Regulations were much more relaxed then, or should I say non-existent. Mine owners held the whip hand and dictated conditions, which were usually very bad.'

'But what about the families?' replied Madeleine. 'George had a family of five children.

How did they manage? One of them was only eighteen months old. She would have grown up never knowing her father. Didn't they care? Didn't they feel any sense of responsibility?' Madeleine's socialist roots were now beginning to show as she became more agitated.

'It was like that in so many industries, mining, steel-making, cotton, wool and pottery to name but a few,' said Tim. 'Labour was cheap, and profit was king. Generally speaking the owners made as much money as possible by paying wages as low as they could get away with. There were the odd exceptions, the Rowntree family, and William Lever were two, but they were very unusual. When the man of the house died, families had to do the best they could. Women often married again, of course, if they could, to replace the breadwinner for the family. Otherwise it was likely to be the workhouse. And if the wife died, then the husband would remarry to provide a mother for his children. Divorce was unknown for the vast majority of the population, so women and men in unhappy relationships had to put up with them. People died younger so these situations often resolved themselves. Different times from today.'

'Yes, I suppose so, doesn't make it right, though, does it?'

Madeleine continued;

'Interesting though, to have such an event in the family. George was Granddad's mother's father. His wife must have had a hard time of it. It looks as though she didn't remarry, but managed to bring up her family through cleaning and taking in washing. A common enough story, I'm afraid. But even at this distance in time George's death is very sad. What a waste of a life, and what hardship brought upon that family, and many others, just through greed. Imagine those little children, Daddy not coming home from work one day. It's just so sad'

Tim stopped and stared.

All of a sudden his thoughts went back to twenty years ago when he was working at Emberton Borough Council, and the attractive, married brunette he had struck up a friendship with. He remembered his daughter, whom he had never seen, but whose name he knew, and he realised that she would now be an adult. He speculated what she might be like. Dark probably, like him and her mother, and not as tall as other girls perhaps; neither he nor her mother were especially tall. This period in his life was not one on which Tim liked to dwell; it held too many unhappy memories. Madeleine's story of great-great granddad George had brought it back to mind. It pained him to think of daughters growing up without their fathers.

She had been outgoing and easy to talk to; she also, he recalled, had a husband who apparently did not appreciate her. As a rule Tim did not like being involved with married women. They brought too many problems with them, and indeed Deborah

Downing was the only married woman he had ever been out with. He had met her at work, on an internal course for council employees, and there had immediately been something which drew them together. It was not that they had common interests particularly, but they felt a bond between them which was indefinable, but very real. Certainly to him, though, Deborah was something special. Tim started to make sure he bumped into Deborah regularly at work, although she worked in a different department, and they began to see each other outside work as well.

Her husband, Michael, was a keen athlete, or had been in his younger days, and he spent at least two evenings a week at the Emberton Runners Athletic Club, training youngsters. It was on these evenings that Tim and Deborah began to see more and more of each other. Deborah had lived at home with her widowed, elderly mother, who had been ill for a number of years. Michael had moved in with Deborah, and they had cared for her together and shortly after Deborah's mother died she and Michael married.

That was in 1987 and Tim and Deborah had not met until she and Michael had been married for nearly four years. Deborah always said that during those four years she had become more of a doormat to Michael than she ever was before they married. She'd told him how Michael was a spendthrift and that she had to keep a sharp eye on the money, or he would spend it without thinking. She had also felt deserted by him as he was so often at the 'Runners', as he called it.

Tim was a good listener and a welcome shoulder to cry on. He was similarly careful about how he spent his money, although he did not consider himself mean, just that he did not spend money he did not have. Her outlook on life seemed very similar to his, and a relationship developed whereby they almost knew what each other were feeling and thinking without having to say so. This natural affinity and comfort between them developed into a more intimate relationship, and Deborah and Tim were soon spending more and more time together.

Deborah told Tim that she was convinced that

Michael was having an affair with someone he knew from work, but she was never sure of the details. She also said that she was concerned that Michael's reason for marrying her in the first place was not the one that a woman might hope for. He had always seemed too interested in her mother's financial affairs, and after she died Michael was even more profligate, and Deborah had found it a struggle to keep his spending under control. His own parents were very ill, and needed nursing home fees to be paid. Deborah understood that, but she was reluctant to spend her mother's money on paying for Michael's parents' fees, when he said he could not afford to fund them himself, and when his brother refused point blank to have anything to do with them.

Just over a year after they had started their relationship, Deborah told Tim that she was pregnant. Tim was delighted and immediately suggested to Deborah that she should leave her husband and come to live with him, start divorce proceedings and they would marry as soon as the divorce came through. Deborah, however, declined the offer, saying that she could not be absolutely certain that the child was his. Tim was distraught, as he had not realised that Deborah was still sleeping with her husband, but he repeated the suggestion. Deborah said that she would think about it and let him know. In the meantime she promised she would continue to see him. She did, however, leave work early in the pregnancy, at Michael's suggestion, and this gave fewer opportunities for Tim to see her. It was also more difficult out of work, as Michael was now taking a greater interest in her, spending less time out at the Athletics Club and more time at home.

As the pregnancy progressed, Tim saw less and less of Deborah, although on the occasions they spoke he still expressed the view that he would like to marry her. She did tell him that she was 99 per cent certain that he was the father, and she said she would let him know when the baby was born. Apparently Michael continued to take a great deal of interest in the pregnancy, although, according to Deborah, he was unaware that it was unlikely that he was the father. When the baby was born Deborah telephoned Tim and told him that she had had a little girl, and she was going to call her Grace. He was overjoyed and again repeated his offer of marriage and support, which she still declined. She said that it was the wrong time to be making such a big decision, but Tim was getting the impression that she had finally decided to stay with Michael. If the baby really was his, he could not see why she would make this decision. When he tried to contact her subsequently he was unsuccessful, with telephone calls not being answered and letters returned 'gone away'. With this, Tim came to the conclusion that his previous thoughts were correct and Deborah was staying with Michael. Maybe she had calculated that the baby was Michael's after all. Then he learned that she and Michael had left the district, and he was unable to find where they had gone to. She had left the council when she was first pregnant and they would not, or could not, disclose any forwarding address. This seemed to be the end of the story, and it was only Madeleine's discoveries which had brought it all back.

'Tim. Penny for them.' Madeleine recalled Tim back from his past.

'Sorry, Madeleine. I was miles away. I was thinking about what you were saying about a little girl who's daddy didn't come home one day. My little girl never had her real daddy coming home to her, did she?'

Madeleine knew all about Tim and Deborah, and she had been sorry that they had not married. Tim had been very distressed when Deborah cut him off like she did, and she, Madeleine, had spent a lot of time with Tim to help him through what had become almost a bereavement for him. As the years had gone by Tim mentioned Deborah less and less, and it was some years now since any reference had been made to her or Grace. Madeleine had thought that that was for the best, although Richard had said that Tim should not hide away from his feelings in the matter.

'I suppose you could trace her now, couldn't you?' asked Madeleine.

'I don't know. It's not that I was ever confirmed as the father anyway. If Deborah had been sleeping with both of us at the same time, there's no guarantee that I am the father. Even if I found her I could hardly turn up one day to a total stranger and say, "by the way I might be your father, would you take a test just in case?" could I?'

'No, I wasn't meaning that,' said Madeleine, 'but you could buy a copy of her birth certificate, for example, and see whom she names as the father, and what other details she puts on there. Who registered the birth? Where did she have the baby? In hospital or at home?

'I'm not sure; I think it was at home. Michael became very protective towards the end of the pregnancy and said he wanted to look after her himself. It always struck me as a little odd; you would think that if he wanted to take care of her, he would have wanted to have medical help on hand in a maternity unit or hospital. I can't think it very likely she would name me as the father if she was planning to stay with Michael, do you?'

'No, probably not,' replied Madeleine. 'But it is only just under a tenner to buy the certificate. Why don't you do that just to see? You never know. I am always telling people there are constant surprises in this family history business. As she is the age she is you will have to give her exact date of birth to be able to buy a certificate; do you know that?'

'Yes, I certainly do. My only child; of course I know her birthday; 11 March 1993. I have often wished I could send her a card but even if I knew her address, she knows nothing about me and Deborah probably wants to keep her parentage a secret.'

'I'll order a copy for you now,' said Madeleine. 'Come on.'

Madeleine led Tim through into the living room where she switched on her computer and logged on to the Births, Marriages and Deaths website. She keyed in the appropriate details and waited for the response. When she saw it she was taken aback.

'What was Deborah's maiden name, Tim? Was it Baxter?'

'Why?'

Madeleine showed Tim the result of her search. Grace Downing registered in the March of 1993, mother's maiden name Baxter, and Victoria Downing, same registration month, same mother's maiden name.

'I don't know for sure.' continued Tim. 'I didn't think so, but I don't know that she ever told me. But who is Victoria Downing? I wonder if Deborah had twins. She never said. Surely she would have told me if I was the father of twins. You'd better send for both certificates, let's see what they might tell us.'

Madeleine agreed and placed the order and told Tim that he would now have to wait a week or so before finding the answer. He was not impressed as he wanted to know now, but Madeleine told him he would have to be patient. Tim was already thinking ahead. How could he trace her if he wanted to? What would be her response to an approach from him? And what would Deborah think, twenty years later? It was a daunting prospect. Maybe he wouldn't go through with it after all; it might only bring heartbreak where there had been none. He thought he would reconsider next week, when he had seen the birth certificates, and what they had to tell him.

Madeleine returned to the kitchen and the coffee, which was now stone cold.

'I'll put the kettle on again, Tim, sorry about that,'

They both looked out of the window and saw the rain, falling like stair rods. Tim dashed out of the back door and picked up his hedge-trimmer, which he had left on the patio. He hurried into the garage where he carefully wiped it down before wrapping the oily rag around it to keep it protected against rust. He was very careful to look after his garden tools; he did not want them to let him down at a vital moment. He returned to the kitchen where there was another steaming cup of coffee awaiting him, which he was not going to let go cold this time. Smiling at Madeleine, he sat down and waited for another biscuit.

Planning applications crossed his desk and were commented upon and reported on, meetings were attended and planning officers briefed. More hedges were trimmed and trees cut, but despite all this that was going on in his life Tim Lock only had thoughts for one thing, his daughter's birth certificate.

Madeleine told him it would be a week or so before it arrived, but Tim was hopeful that it would be sooner. Each morning he would check the post, if it arrived before he left for work, or he would ask Madeleine to telephone him as soon as the postman had been. Tim realised he was becoming obsessed, but he could not help it. Ever since his conversation with Madeleine he had been thinking about Deborah and little Grace. How was she? How had she grown up? Who did she look like? He knew that none of these questions would be answered by the birth certificate, but they were all prompted by the ordering of it.

It was a Friday morning and it was nearly two weeks since Madeleine had ordered the birth certificate. Just as he was walking out to the car he saw the postman at the far end of the road. He was tempted to wait to see what might come, but he had an important meeting first thing at work and he did not want to be late. He reversed his car out of the drive, and set off for work. As he passed the postman he was still half a dozen doors away, so it would not have been possible to wait that long. He would have to check with Madeleine as soon as possible. It was a dreary, grey day as he drove the familiar route to the planning office. He parked in his allotted place and walked in through the swing doors of the council offices. He acknowledged Sarah on the reception desk, as he usually did, and walked up two flights of stairs to his office. He picked up a coffee from the machine on the landing and went to his desk to collect the papers for his morning meeting. He glanced at the clock, and it read two minutes to nine. He was trying to decide whether he would have time to telephone home before the meeting, scheduled for 9.15, when his boss, Tony Grant, called to him.

'Morning, Tim, can you spare me a moment before the meeting. Just one or two things I wanted to go over with you.'

'Sure,' replied Tim, 'Just coming.'

That put paid to any idea he might have about telephoning Madeleine. It would have to wait. He and Tony went along to the meeting together. It seemed to drag on for ever. It was bad enough normally, but with this hanging over him Tim could not wait for it to be over. As a result, when Tony Grant asked him for a point of view on a particular matter, he was caught unprepared and fumbled for an answer, which was most unlike him, and which he thought would have been noticed. He was annoyed with himself and apologised to Tony after the meeting, but inwardly he cursed having to attend such a gathering when the more important matter of his daughter was still outstanding.

His lunch break arrived none too soon and Tim rushed out to his car so that he could ring Madeleine in private. He took out his mobile and punched in the numbers, his hands shaking as he did so. Madeleine picked up the receiver immediately.

'Hello, Tim. No, they haven't come, neither Grace's nor Victoria's. I've had an email from the register office, or whoever sends these certificates out, saying that there is no one with the details you gave born at that time.'

'What could be wrong? Can you check the details on the applications, to make sure we filled in the right information and didn't make any spelling mistakes?' said Tim.

'Yes, I have already done that. No spelling mistakes.'

'We weren't sure about Deborah's maiden name, were we? Maybe it's not the right Grace

Downing. I don't know. We'll have a think when I come home. I've got to go. Bye.'

Tim ended the call and sat in his car, unable to comprehend what Madeleine had just said to him. In his own mind he was convinced that birth, or at least Grace's, was 'his' daughter, so why did the details not match? He got out of the car, locked it and walked slowly back into the building, deep in thought. Over lunch he was unnaturally quiet, and his colleagues wondered whether he had received some bad news, but they did not like to pry.

Madeleine put down the telephone and also started to go over various possibilities. She would have to do some detective work before Tim came home later, when they could consider it together.

In Tim's office the clock seemed to be on a go-slow. The afternoon dragged by and Tim stared distractedly out of the window at the scudding clouds and swirling wind. Concentration would just not come, and when five o'clock arrived he hurried down the stairs to his car, and drove away before anyone could stop him. The weather had not improved during the day and the Friday night traffic was as bad as ever. Eventually he pulled into his driveway, and locking the car he went quickly indoors. Tim had been puzzling over the email all afternoon. He could not see why the register office had said what they had. What could he and Madeleine have possibly got wrong?

'Let's have a look,' he said to Madeleine, who had already printed off the email for him to see.

'What have we got wrong?' he continued, 'There just can't be two Grace Downings born at the same time. Where does Victoria fit in? What do we definitely know? We know her name was Grace. We assume her father would have been registered as Michael Downing. We know her date of birth. We know her mother was Deborah Downing. We know her place of birth. There isn't anything else.'

'What about the maiden name?' asked Madeleine, 'We know what it says on the birth index, Baxter, but you said that you didn't know Deborah's maiden name. When we ordered the certificate we had to give the mother's first name. Maybe it wasn't Deborah. Was Deborah her first or second Christian name? If her name was, I don't know, Christine Deborah, maybe that would account for the certificate not being sent, do you think?'

Madeleine was struggling for an explanation. In her research into other members of the family this was not a problem she had encountered before. She had had emails declining to issue certificates previously, but those were always for reasons that she was aware of, times when she had taken a gamble on details, hoping them to be right. This time she was sure of the information which she had provided, and that was what made this particularly difficult. She could not work out which piece of information was incorrect, and the email did not tell her.

Now it was Tim's turn to try to make sense of this problem.

'She never said so. It's possible, I suppose. We could look for Michael's marriage to Deborah. Would that tell us her maiden name and if she had another name?'

Madeleine turned to her computer and started searching. She soon found a Michael Downing marrying a Deborah Roberts in 1987.

'Look, Tim, his wife's maiden name is Roberts not Baxter. And look at this' she said excitedly. 'Who is this marrying Louise Baxter in 1993? If it isn't Michael Downing.'

'Just a minute,' said Tim, defensively. 'I know

that Deborah Downing had a little girl, she told me. She also told me that her name was Grace. What's going on?'

'Did you ever see her after the baby was born?' asked Madeleine.

Tim thought for a moment.

'No, I didn't, but we spoke on the phone. That's how I know about the baby details.'

Madeleine walked back out into the kitchen. She wanted to check on the meal she was cooking, but also to have a moment or two on her own before confronting Tim with something she had thought about during the afternoon. It was not going to be easy, so she decided to continue with the cooking and leave it until they had eaten, and Tim had had a chance to contemplate things for himself.

The lamb chops, Jersey potatoes, fresh vegetables and mint sauce were just to Tim's liking, and Madeleine's come to that. Madeleine had bought a bottle of red wine to accompany the meal, and she hoped that Tim would be in a more receptive frame of mind after eating. The meal proceeded without any further discussion on the subject of Deborah and Grace. Tim seemed lost in his own thoughts, and Madeleine wanted to leave it for the time being. She made fresh coffee and brought it through into the living room, where Tim was sitting, looking distractedly at the printed email.

'Now, Tim,' she began, 'I've been thinking.'

'What?' snapped Tim, still irritated by the inconvenient information in the email.

'Don't shoot the messenger, Tim.'

'Sorry, Madeleine, it's just that I can't understand. If Grace is Deborah's daughter, then why is Louise Baxter, and I am making an assumption that it is the same woman as in that marriage, named as the mother? Anyway, what have you been thinking?'

'I am thinking that you did not see Deborah after the birth, and that she said she didn't want to leave Michael for you, despite what you had told me about how he treated her. What if she couldn't leave him?'

'I don't understand, what do you mean?'

'If Michael was holding her against her will, then she ran away, leaving her baby behind. Maybe the baby was not yours, and Deborah knew it. Michael then marries this Louise, and pretends that Grace is hers.'

Madeleine had been speculating during the afternoon that Tim had been the victim of a cruel hoax.

'No, I don't think so. Deborah was thrilled to be pregnant, and thrilled that it was my baby, and was really looking forward to the birth. She was confident that I was the father, and she explained why. It was almost impossible for Michael to be the father. She wouldn't run away and leave her little girl, I am confident of that. Anyway, even if she did, she would have come to me. But I very much got the impression at the time that Deborah and Michael were trying to make a go of it, and that was why she wouldn't come away with me.'

'Then why did he marry Louise? Why don't we order the marriage certificate for Michael and Louise and see what that might tell us?'

'I am not sure it is going to tell us anything, but then we didn't think that Grace's birth certificate was going to either, and look what's happened there. We might as well give it a try,' said Tim. 'Get it back on the screen. Let's have a look at the details.'

Madeleine keyed in the information – marriage of Michael Downing in the five years either side of 1992. She was surprised at the results. Michael Downing, marrying Deborah Roberts in Emberton in 1987, Louise Baxter in Hopley in 1993, and Fiona Lewis in Hopley in1997.

'Emberton is where the two girls were born, but the maiden name of the mother was Baxter.

Goodness me! He's addicted to marriage. Who are all these women who find him so irresistible? Better order all three, I think. And while we are about it we might as well have another try for Grace, let's try Louise Baxter as the mother, see what that brings,' said Madeleine.

Her previous life as a vicar's wife had inured her to most of life's unexpected events, but she could not remember coming across someone who had been married so often in such as short period of time before.

Tim was speechless. However many women Michael Downing had married, assuming it was the same Michael Downing, it did not explain what had happened to Deborah and Grace, and that was all he was really interested in. Hopefully, he thought, they will send Grace's birth certificate this time. He took another gulp of the coffee, draining the cup, then he stood up and walked over to the sideboard, and taking out a bottle of whisky and a glass, poured himself a large one.

'I think I could do with this. It's been quite a day.'

'Two glasses, then,' said Madeleine. 'It's not every day that you come across a serial bigamist.'

'Or worse' said Tim, half under his breath.

Paula was sitting comfortably in her chair in Fiona's kitchen, coffee at her side. Fiona had been to Ian's funeral on Wednesday and it was now Friday morning. Michael was busy in the shop and this was the first opportunity that the two women had to get together to talk about what Fiona had learned. She had been very quiet since returning, and conversation with Michael was becoming more and more difficult. It seemed to her that the more she discovered through her family tree research, the more worried she became about what remained to be unearthed. She was a bright, friendly personality by nature and she wanted to find the best in people, and she was finding this more difficult with Michael as time went by. Their personal relationship was suffering as well, she had always enjoyed the physical side of their marriage, but she was finding it more awkward to be intimate with a man she was beginning to suspect was not all she hoped he was. Michael was starting to notice this change as well. His normal charming exterior was giving way to an irritable manner over trivial matters. He was resenting the time Fiona was spending with Paula, and the apparent secretive nature of their conversations. He was also missing the girls; they had been back at university two or three weeks and had hardly been in touch. He kept telling himself that they were growing up and starting to lead their own lives, but this was not helping his overall demeanour. Although Fiona had noticed the change in Michael she did not think that it was because he had guessed that she had found out secrets from his past. She put it down to his not having his family around him; they were, after all, his only link with Louise, whom she was convinced, was the big love of his life.

'Come on, then,' said Paula. 'What have you got to tell me?'

Fiona had already told her briefly on the telephone about the funeral but Paula wanted the full details

'To start with,' replied Fiona, 'I was not

surprised that Michael did not want to go. He spoke quite sharply about Linda, so while he was clearly upset at the news of his brother's death, there still seemed to be bad feeling between them. He didn't even want to write a letter of condolence, so I wrote and said that Michael had an appointment at the hospital which he couldn't break. I also explained that I was his second wife and that his first wife had been killed in a car crash. I thought it was a poor excuse for not going to your own brother's funeral, but there it is.'

'However, I am pleased that I did go. It was a reverent service, and then I went back to the house afterwards for a drink. I met Linda, Ian's widow, and she seemed pleased to see me, although after my letter, she had not been expecting me. She introduced me briefly to her three sons, well to one really, and she pointed the other two out. It was all very normal, until she asked me about Deborah. Linda clearly thought that Deborah was the accident victim, and she asked about the baby. Apparently she was pregnant the last time they met, about five months. I pretended that one of the twins was the baby, and swiftly got off the subject. Fortunately it did not arise again. I was not able to find out when this pregnancy was, so I don't know the outcome of it, but she would have been too far gone for a miscarriage, surely?'

'Yes, she would. And if you are right, who is the baby, because whoever it is, is grown up now?'

'I might have an answer for that,' said Fiona. 'When I came home I had another look at the twins' birth certificates. Here they are.'

She handed them to Paula for her to have a look.

'We've looked at these before, Fi,' said Paula, 'What's new?'

Fiona pointed out the registration details to

Paula.

'Look at these dates. Michael Downing has registered both births, with the same father, mother, place of birth and everything else. But while the date of birth is the same, the date of the registration is different, Victoria on the ninth of March, and Grace on the thirteenth. Now why would he do that?'

'I don't know,' admitted Paula.

'When the girls were born, if they had been twins, Michael would have registered them on the same day, with the same details, and he would have been asked the time of birth, to establish which twin was the older. If the girls were not twins, he wouldn't be asked to give that information, and he was probably unaware of the necessity for it.'

'For whatever reason, he clearly returned on a different day, making sure there was a different registrar on duty so he wasn't remembered. There seems no logic to it.'

'One thing is certain,' said Paula. 'Or least I think it is, and that is that Grace and Victoria are not twins, but only half-sisters. I bet that Deborah is the mother of one of them and Louise the other.'

'But which is which?' asked Fiona. 'I would guess that Victoria is Louise's, she looks similar, tallish and fair. I remember Sam Wainwright saying that Deborah was dark, and that would fit with her being Grace's mother. In which case I think that the date on the birth certificates is definitely Victoria's birthday, because Louise would have made sure she celebrated her birthday on the right day. We don't know for sure when Grace was born, it could have been the same day, or earlier, or even a few days later. He registered Victoria's birth first, so I would guess that if they were born on different days, then Victoria is the older, but it can only be by a few days.'

'So what you are saying,' said Paula, 'is that Michael's wife, Deborah, was pregnant with Grace and Michael's lover, Louise, was pregnant with Victoria at the same time, and they gave birth on the same day, or within a few days of each other.'

'Yes,' said Fiona, 'That seems most likely.'

'So is that what Sam Wainwright knew and wanted to talk to Michael about?' added Paula, 'it's no wonder Michael was worried about talking to him.'

'Maybe, I wonder if he just knew he was married to Deborah, not about the pregnancy. I think he would have mentioned that when he spoke to you, don't you think?'

'Possibly, but if he did know he may have wanted to keep that information to tell Michael himself.'

Fiona and Paula looked at each other in disbelief. Weeks of trying to do something beneficial for Grace and Victoria had ended like this. Fiona was wondering how she was going to tell them.

'I need a breath of fresh air,' said Fiona.

She walked out through the kitchen door, across the road and into the garden. The snowdrops were starting to appear in the borders, and although it was only the end of January, Fiona felt that spring was imminent. She only wished that she felt more like welcoming it. She walked down towards the trees at the end of the garden, and was joined by Paula, who had stopped to put a coat on.

'Remember I said to you when the girls went away in October about nostalgia. It's all come tumbling down. It's all been a fantasy. Michael, the twins, our marriage, it's all a sham. How can I ever feel the same again?'

Tears formed in her eyes as she screwed them up against the wind. Paula put her arms around her.

'Come on, let's get back inside. You have done nothing wrong. You've been a good mother to those girls, and a good wife to Michael. And he's been good to you as well, whatever happened in the past, hasn't he?'

Fiona was fighting back the tears and failing as she walked back to the flat.

'But how can I feel anything ever again. After doing that to those two women and those girls. Pretending they were twins when they weren't. What was the point?'

Paula opened the door and ushered Fiona back into the kitchen. She reached over and picked up the kettle to boil some fresh water for a cup of tea.

'Let's look to the future,' said Paula. 'That's what we need to do. Now how are we going to find Deborah? She should be able to tell us everything and we can also reunite her with her daughter.'

'That's assuming she's still around,' said Fiona. 'She could be anywhere. If she and Michael split up she might have found someone else, emigrated, who knows?'

'She could even be dead,' she added, gloomily.

'Let's look at this logically. We don't know exactly when Grace was born, assuming that Michael lied on the certificate, but we know he married when?'

Fiona opened her folder and took out the marriage certificate of Louise and Michael.

'14 April 1993.'

'So by then Grace has been born and Deborah

is out of the picture. If Grace was born, let's say, on 10 March; that gives five weeks for something to happen. Grace was born at Emberton and the marriage took place here in Hopley, so they had to move as well in that time.'

'Why don't we advertise to see if we can make contact with Deborah? We could write to the local press, for example, saying we are tracing lost relatives for a family tree. I've seen those sorts of letters in local papers before.' said Fiona.

'That's more positive. Good idea,' Paula agreed. 'We could also advertise on the Internet. There are social networking sites that are devoted to family history, and people often advertise on those for lost relatives as well. There were details in that book I had out of the library, I'll get it again.'

Fiona had dried her tears now and was feeling a little better. Paula made her a cup of tea, which she drank gratefully. She was now feeling more positive, although she could not forget what she had recently found out about her husband, and was not sure she was going to be able to forgive him either. She was very fond of the girls, and she could not bear the thought of hurting them for reasons which were not anything to do with them.

'Why don't I pop to the library and see if I can borrow it again. I'll come back this afternoon and we will do it. Are you ok now?'

Fiona nodded.

'Yes, I'll be fine. I'll see you later.'

Paula went out of the kitchen door, not wishing to walk through the shop and see Michael. Fiona slipped upstairs to redo her make-up, not wanting Michael to see that she had been crying. All this time Michael, oblivious to everything that had been going on, was busy in the shop. He was very committed to his business, and would be reluctant to let anything spoil his carefully constructed world. In his mind the past was the past, and it was best for it to stay there. Whatever had happened he did not want resurrected, and that was why he was not keen on Fiona's project with the family history, but it had been very difficult for him to prevent her doing her investigations. That would only entail him having to explain why he was not in favour of it.

Paula returned after lunch, and came once again to the kitchen door to avoid Michael, clutching the library book.

'Here we are,' she said, handing the book over to Fiona, who was still sitting quietly at the table, having just eaten a sandwich for lunch. Fiona flicked through the book and found the section which listed various useful website addresses for family historians. She jotted down two addresses which seemed to be the best for their purpose, closed the book, and said to Paula;

'Right, what shall we say?'

'Something along the lines of "I am

researching my family tree and would like to contact Deborah Downing, nee Roberts, last heard of in Emberton in 1993". Then give your email address.'

'Yes, that's good. Let's do it.'

Fiona logged on to the website and registered as a new user on the site. She then placed the advert as they had decided and they both hoped for an early reply.

'What about the papers? What is the local paper back in Emberton?' asked Paula.

'I don't know, but the Internet is a wonderful thing, I'm sure we can find out. Fiona googled 'Emberton newspapers' and there it was, the , complete with telephone number and address.

'We'll write to them along the same lines,' said Paula.

'OK.'

Fiona took out a piece of writing paper, and carefully composed the letter. She thought it would be better to use her maiden name as she didn't want to be requesting information on someone named Downing, having given her own name as Downing. She also wanted to avoid indicating that there would be any financial benefit in replying.

'I'll post that on my way home.'

'Thanks, Paula. Now, there is something else I would value your opinion on. With all that has been going on recently I need to speak to the girls. I can't leave it forever. How do you think I should deal with it? Should I go up and see them?'

'Is it a bit soon? We haven't got much in the way of definite information. It's all a bit sketchy. Mind you, if they come home you won't have the opportunity with Michael being around.'

Paula paused.

'Yes, go on then, take a day and go and spend it with them, but make sure you tell them you are not sure about various bits. You will have to arrange it in advance. It will be difficult, though. How do you think they will take it?'

'I'm not sure. I think Victoria should be ok, but Grace might be different. Of course a lot depends on whether we get any response to our adverts. I'll go and have a word with Michael, because I'll have to fix the day with him.'

Fiona went through to the shop where Michael was browsing through publishers' catalogues, deciding on new purchases.

'Michael, I think I'll phone the girls and arrange a day up in Birmingham. We could go and have a girlie day shopping, and they can show me around.'

'Sounds good. When are you thinking of going?'

'Well, which day would suit you best?'

'Have a word with the girls, but next Friday is probably best for me.'

Michael was very relaxed; he was always at his best in the shop, surrounded by his business.

'Let me know.'

Fiona went back to the flat and rang Grace. She answered almost straight away.

'Hello, Mum. Oooh, what a super idea, I'm sure Vicky will think so too,' she said when Fiona explained her plan. Fiona suggested the Friday as Michael had said and Grace said that she was free most of that day, and she was fairly sure that Vicky was too.

'I'll check now with Vicky and text you,' she said.

A few moments later Fiona's mobile buzzed in her handbag. Reaching it out, she read the message. Grace suggested that Fiona should catch the train to save her the trouble of driving into the centre of the city, and they would meet up at New Street Station at 10.30am. Fiona replied immediately and said how much she was looking forward to it. She did not say how much she was dreading it at the same time. Walking back into the shop she told Michael what she had agreed with the twins, and he was pleased that she was going to see them.

'Have you done anything more for those folders you gave them at Christmas?' he said

'No, nothing really. I am still finding out bits and pieces for myself.' Fiona felt dreadful lying to Michael in this way, but did not feel able to disclose to him all the information that had been coming her way.

There would be time enough, she thought, to talk to him at length on the subject. Michael turned back to his catalogues and Fiona disappeared back to the flat. She was still finding it difficult to come to terms with what she had learned at the funeral, and the subsequent discovery about the registration dates with Paula. Her eyes filled with tears again as she thought once more of those girls growing up, and how Michael had deceived them, and her. Paula was the one person who she could really rely on; without her she did not think she would be able to cope. Her friend hugged her as she came back to the flat.

'I've told Michael and he's happy for me to go. Wish me luck.' Fiona said.

Paula smiled.

'You'll be fine, and don't worry. The girls are great; they're young enough to get over anything.'

Fiona managed a tearful smile as Paula left to go home. She hoped she was right.

Madeleine had been a vicar's wife for many years, and although she was now in a different parish, she was still closely involved with the Church. One of the tasks she now undertook was guiding visitors through the Church's records of Births, Marriages and Deaths. The registers were kept in the safe in the vestry, and when family tree researchers contacted the rector he would put them on to Madeleine. She had met a variety of people doing this work and they all had different stories to tell; of missing sons, daughters and parents; of ancestors who had lived in the same parish for generations; and of rogues and thieves, looking to escape justice, but who had ended up in the churchyard like everyone else. Among all the tales she had heard though, she thought there was nothing to compare with Tim's sad tale of betrayal and injustice.

At least that was how she saw it. Tim was still waiting for the certificates which he had sent for recently, and which would confirm or otherwise his worst fears.

Following the discoveries they had made Tim had found it difficult to get back to normal. He was so taken up with establishing the truth about Deborah and Grace that he had become morose and silent, lost in his own thoughts much of the time. Each day, therefore, it was with some trepidation that Madeleine watched the postman walking up to their front door; each day expecting news that she was not sure would be good.

Every morning Tim went off to work disappointed if the post had not arrived. He was becoming obsessed. Then one morning Madeleine heard the clunk of the letterbox and walked through to the hall to pick up the delivery. There was a white envelope which apparently contained what they were both waiting for. It was only just past nine o'clock, so she could ring Tim before his day really started. She left the envelope unopened until she had spoken to him. Picking up the telephone she punched in his direct line number at the Council.

'Tim Lock, Planning,' he answered.

'Tim. I have what looks like an interesting envelope. What do you want me to do?'

'Can you bear not to open it?' he said.

Tim thought, he could not go back home, much as he might like to, and he really wanted to open it for himself.

'For you, Tim, of course. I shall put it somewhere where I can't be tempted. I'll see you later, bye.'

Madeleine put down the phone, rather disappointed. She had hoped that Tim would let her open the envelope; it was, after all, she reasoned, she who had set this whole thing in motion. Having said that, though, if the news was not good, it would be better for Tim to receive it at home, rather than over the phone at work. Madeleine put the envelope on the dresser in the kitchen and continued with her day, but each time she went into and out of the room the envelope was staring at her, daring her to open it.

Eventually she could stand it no longer and she picked it up and went through into the living room. She sat down and stared at it, but she could not do it, and she put it down on the coffee table, and left it behind.

Tim's days always seemed long to him now, and this one seemed longer than ever. He was becoming more and more disenchanted with his job, and with the Council. He wished he could take early retirement and concentrate on his garden. He dreamed of having an allotment, growing his own vegetables and fruit, and not being beholden to what he was now seeing as petty bureaucracy that prevented him doing his job properly. These would have to remain dreams for the moment, but, he thought, you never know what might be just around the corner. Eventually the office clock struggled its way to five o'clock and the place emptied in less than ten minutes. Tim locked up and went down to the car park, got into his car and drove home expectantly He had been waiting for these items to come for a week or more, but now he was anxious about seeing them. He wasn't sure why, only that for the last nineteen years he had barely thought of Deborah and Grace, and now they were about to be back in his life.

As he pulled into the drive he saw Madeleine waiting at the window. He knew thatshe would not have opened the envelope; she was much too honest for that. He trusted her implicitly. He put his key in the door and as he opened it Madeleine said;

'Come on, Tim, I've been waiting all day, and that envelope has been daring me to open it.'

Tim walked into the small hall, put down his briefcase and took off his shoes.

'Where is it then?' he asked.

'Here.' She handed it to him and he tore it open.

Inside there were three marriage certificates, those of Deborah, Louise and Fiona, but not the two birth certificates of Victoria and Grace which they had ordered. He glanced at the green marriage certificates and then went into the living room and sat down. Putting on his spectacles he had a closer look. He noticed that Michael had called himself a bachelor on Deborah's and Louise's and a widower on Fiona's. He handed them across to Madeleine.

'What do you make of that?' he asked.

Madeleine looked closely.

'On both his marriage to Deborah and Louise he says he's a bachelor. He can't be a bachelor twice,' she said, 'and when he says he's a widower, who's died?'

'Louise, I suppose,' said Tim. 'Anyway, never mind about that now, where are the birth certificates? Why haven't they come?'

'I don't know,' replied Madeleine. 'I thought we had the right information this time. I wonder if we've had an email about it. Let me go and have a look.'

Madeleine went across to her computer and checked her email.

'Here we are,' she said. 'The certificates have not been provided because the birth dates supplied were incorrect, it says here. You knew Grace's birthday though, didn't you?'

'Yes, of course, I don't understand what is going on here,' replied Tim. 'She was born on 11 March 1993. That's definite. Deborah told me herself. I am totally baffled.'

Tim slumped back into his chair. His face clouded over and he snapped;

'What's going on? Why has my baby been left out? Somebody is up to something and I intend to find out who and what.'

Madeleine walked across the room and poured him a large whisky.

'Calm down Tim, get this down you and we'll have a think. I'm sure we can sort it out.'

Madeleine was always the more placid of the two, and knew how to deal with Tim's occasional rages.

Tim took the glass gratefully and downed it in almost one swallow.

'You're the expert, then,' he said to his sister. 'What's the answer?'

'Well. To start with I am sure that we have ordered the right birth certificate. I am sure that it is Grace. I know you said that Deborah let you know when Grace was born, but is it possible that she phoned you the day after, so that her birthday was really the 10 not the 11? That could account for the discrepancy.'

'I don't think so, I can't be sure, I suppose. She said that she had had her baby that morning, so unless she was not telling the truth, it seems fairly certain. But what about the other baby, Victoria? Whose is she, and have we got her birthday wrong as well. Like I said, Deborah never mentioned to me anything about having had twins. Surely she would have said. Could there be any other reason or reasons why the birth dates would be wrong?'

'If whoever registered the birth just gave the wrong date, either accidently or deliberately, perhaps.'

'I can't see anyone doing it accidentally. The birth of your baby is too important to get it wrong. But why would you do it deliberately?' asked Tim.

'It just depends what you may want to cover up. What has Michael got to hide? Grace's parentage?

I can't see why giving an incorrect date of birth would cover that up, but there doesn't seem to be anything else. What do those marriage certificates tell us?'

'I see that Michael Downing married Louise Baxter in April after these girls were born. We know from the birth records that they were both born in March. That means he's told yet another lie on this certificate. There is a maiden name listed on the birth indices, so he must have said that the mother was married, otherwise the birth name and maiden name would be the same. I really don't see the point. Who is or was Louise Baxter? We know nothing about her.'

'When we were looking the other day, and you were telling me about Michael Downing, you said that Deborah thought he had been having an affair with someone at work. Could this have been her?' said Madeleine.

'Possibly,' replied Tim. 'I don't know, but hold on; on the marriage certificate it gives her occupation. What does it say?'

Madeleine looked over his shoulder

'Bookseller, but living at the same address. Looks as if they ran a bookshop together.'

'That's no good then,' said Tim. 'We need to find Deborah, that's the main thing. She would be able to tell us what went wrong, and you never know...' he said, with a glint in his eye, '... she might still fancy me.'

Madeleine threw a cushion at him and laughed, pleased to see he had recovered his good temper.

'You're a few years older now; mind you, so is she.'

Madeleine scanned the other marriage

documents.

'It seems as if something happened between Grace being born and Michael and Louise marrying, and then something else between that marriage and the marriage to this Fiona Lewis. It says Michael is a widower, so it looks as though Louise died at some time. We could search to see if there is a death of either a Deborah Downing or a Louise Downing during the relevant period. Of course they might have died elsewhere and then, whilst there would be a death registered, it would not be recognisable as the person we are after.'

'How do you mean?' asked Tim.

'When you die the death is registered in the district in which you die, not where you were living. So, for example, if Deborah died in a train crash in York, then her death would be registered there. If you were then trying to find that death, not knowing the surrounding circumstances, it would be difficult to trace. There may be several Deborah Downings of a similar age dying in different parts of the country, and you wouldn't know that the York one was the one you were interested in. If you didn't find one in the "right" area you might think it wasn't registered at all. You would have to buy all the certificates just to check them out and that could prove expensive.'

'I prefer to look on the bright side and look for Deborah still living. If she left him after Grace was born, she could have gone anywhere.'

'Yes, but I would still like to look at the deaths for that time just in case. There's no point looking elsewhere if we know she's dead. We'll have a look for Louise as well.'

Madeleine logged on to the website and started to search for deaths in the name of Downing in either Emberton or Hopley.

'Bingo! There we are.'

Tim turned round.

'What have you found?'

'Louise Downing died in Hopley October 1996. It even gives her birth date, 17 September 1960. Wonder what happened?'

'Never mind that,' said Tim. 'What about Deborah?'

'There's no Deborah Downing dying in Emberton or Hopley between Grace's birth and Michael's marriage to Louise. But she could have died elsewhere, as I said. She could have left the country, we just don't know. Our dinner will be going cold if we spend any longer on this. We will reconsider after we have eaten.'

Tim put the papers to one side, reluctantly. He

was constantly in two minds about pursuing this. He kept telling himself to leave well alone, but then could not help thinking about it, wondering what had happened and where his ex-lover and child were. They ate in silence, each pondering the possibilities, and wanting not to think about the worst one. As soon as the meal was finished Tim cleared away, stacked the dishwasher and made coffee for them both. He had calmed down now after his initial rage; his anger was often intense but always short-lived.

'What do you think about an allotment?'

Tim's question surprised Madeleine.

'I fancy growing a few more vegetables, maybe some fruit as well. What do you think?'

'Have you got the time?' she replied. 'There's always plenty to do here; you seem to be out there all the time.'

'Yes, I know, but I have been making enquiries

at work, and it may be possible to go part-time. Young Tom Jefferson is very capable and I can see a time coming, with budget cuts looming, when the Council will be wanting to make changes. If I moved to, say, three days a week, I would still be on the same salary but pro-rata, and I could take on the allotment as well.'

Madeleine smiled at him; she could see the excited look in his eyes, the face of someone enthusing over a job, where he hadn't enthused over his own job for a number of years now. When Richard had died she had received a death-in-service payment from the Church, and she had her clergy widow's pension, and even with Tim's income reduced, they would not struggle financially.

'How seriously have you enquired?' she asked, knowing the answer.

'I have spoken to Tony Grant, and he has had a word with HR. I could change at the end of the financial year if I would like to. It would affect my pension entitlement to a small degree, but not much. I got the impression from Tony that the Council would be quite pleased to receive the enquiry.'

'When do you have to let them know for certain?'

'End of February at the latest, but it could be anytime. As soon as I tell them I want to go ahead they will prepare the necessary documentation, and it will take effect on 5 April. However, the allotments won't be ready until June, I think, so there will be a gap when I can have a bit of a break. If you're agreeable I shall tell them tomorrow.'

'It's not up to me, Tim. It's for you to decide. If you're happy then I'm happy.'

'Right then, it's agreed. I shall tell Tony in the morning. I feel better already. This calls for a drink. A celebratory one this time not a calm-yourself-down one.'

He poured himself another Scotch, only a small one this time, and he gave a small one to Madeleine.

'Here's to .'

'

'Now what about Deborah?' said Tim. 'We can't forget her. How can we find her? What miracles of modern science can you conjure up on your machine that will tell us straight away where she is?'

Madeleine pulled a face at him. It was as if they were children again. Tim was behaving as if a load had been lifted from his shoulders, and he was brighter and lighter for it.

'Before we get to her, what about this allotment? Are you sure there are any to be had?'

'Oh, yes. I signed up for one today, after I had spoken to Tony. There are some new ones coming up for rent at the end of Edward Street. I don't work in the planning office for nothing, you know.'

'Tim!' shouted Madeleine in mock horror. 'You little weasel. You knew I'd say yes, didn't you?'

'Well, I sort of guessed.' He said, in equally mock humility.

'Now down to business; Deborah. What can we do, realistically?'

Madeleine explained to Tim that there were different options open to them. They could identify all the Deborah Downings dying at the right time and at the right age, and buy their death certificates. That would be expensive but thorough, she said. They could try to make contact with Michael Downing and ask him what has been going on. It looks as though he is running or has been running a bookshop somewhere in or near Hopley. They could visit and just wander in to see the lie of the land. Tim pointed out that he had never met Michael, and while he had a rough idea of his appearance, that idea was twenty years out of date. This option seemed to be the riskiest one.

Another possible course of action was to advertise. There were a variety of websites which offered family historians the opportunity to contact other people doing similar research. Madeleine explained that you could put your query on-line and hope that someone else was looking for the same piece of information and could share the search with you, or that someone else knew the answer and could tell you what you wanted to know. The only other idea that she had was to write a letter to the local paper, but as Tim had lived in Emberton for a long time he knew many local people, and he did not think that it would produce the desired result.

They decided to use the Internet, although they were not confident that it would be successful. Madeleine thought that as a general rule these websites were more useful for tracing long dead relatives, or those who had moved away long distances, usually overseas. Tim was anxious that they did not encourage cranks who might cause trouble, but Madeleine assured him that there were safeguards in place to prevent this happening. They decided to advertise for anyone with any knowledge of Deborah Downing also known as Deborah Roberts, thinking that it would be better not to include any reference to Grace Downing. The thought did occur to them that Grace could be married by now, and although that seemed an unlikely prospect they did check, but marriage records online only went up to 2005.

Madeleine drafted out an advert, indicating a desire to make contact by email first, and then by meeting subsequently, if appropriate. She logged on to the site, registered as a new user, and placed the advert, not really expecting a reply.

It was not only Michael who was missing having the girls at home. They had been part of Fiona's life for over fourteen years as well. She had babysat them when they were little, and had mothered them as they grew up. Many of their values and much of their outlook on life stemmed from Fiona, and she missed having them around now they were adult. Of course there had been the usual rows that happen in any family, but overall Fiona's relationship with them was good. This was one of the reasons that she had arranged to visit them in Birmingham. The family history side apart, she was just looking forward to a pleasant day out, lots of shopping, a bit of lunch and plenty of chat. As February wore on, the evenings started to be a little lighter and the gloom of winter seemed to be receding. Michael took her down to the railway station in Hopley in time for the 8.32am train, which was scheduled to arrive at Birmingham New Street at 10.28am. She had bought a new winter coat in the January sales and she was glad of it on this cold

February morning. Michael walked through on to the station with her and kissed her as the train pulled in.

'Give my love to Grace and Victoria, have a nice day, don't spend too much.'

Fiona kissed him back.

'I will, I will and I won't.'

She opened the door and climbed in to the train. Fortunately there was a seat near to the window by the door, and she settled in ready for the two hour journey. She waved through the window as the train pulled away, and watched Michael stride out of the station back to his car. As she did so she tried to put aside any thoughts of deceit, bigamy and worse. He was a good man, she kept telling herself, and he had provided a good living, stop undermining him. But as she took her coat off and put it with her small case on the luggage rack, she remembered what was in there, and all the questions came back to her. She had bought a magazine at the station to take her mind off such matters and to help to pass the time. She opened it and started reading an article about organic vegetables, then found her eyelids drooping as she was rocked by the motion of the train. In a few moments she was asleep, leaning gently against the side window.

'Tickets please!'

She woke with a start as the guard walked down the centre of the train, requesting everyone to show their ticket. She fumbled in her handbag and found the piece of orange card. Why was she always so worried she might have lost it? She handed it over, he looked at it gruffly, clipped it and handed it back.

'Thank you. Tickets please!' He disappeared into the next carriage. Fiona gazed out of the window, at the countryside dashing past, taking her towards what? A pleasant day with her daughters, or an angry confrontation? Fiona was not a regular train traveller, and if she could stay awake for long enough she enjoyed the sensation of the train, and the way that it transported you into the centre of towns and cities without the confusion and congestion of car travel.

She cast her mind back to her schooldays, learning about the great Victorian railway engineers, and how they revolutionised the way people lived their lives; fresh farm produce, milk, vegetables and meat being available in the centre of big cities, and the products of the great factories being taken across the country and across the world. The railways brought employment to thousands and pleasure to millions; holidays by the seaside for those who, otherwise, would never see the sea, and holidays in the countryside for those who had never seen a cow.

She was plucked from her school classroom by the sound of an announcement, which she assumed meant they had arrived at Birmingham. The announcer, as usual, was incomprehensible, but the large signs saying Birmingham New Street, helped. She pulled her briefcase down from the luggage rack, picked up her handbag, put on her coat and prepared to leave the train. The train stopped and the doors were opened. She stepped down gingerly on to the platform, which was underground. Looking around she could not see the twins, but she noticed that the train had arrived three minutes early. She walked across to the stairs which led to the main part of the station. At the top she scanned the crowd for a familiar face, and then she saw two at the entrance. She battled her way through the crowd to where Grace and Victoria were standing. After exchanging hugs and kisses she asked;

'Where's the nearest café, I'm dying for a cup of tea?'

'Upstairs again, that'll take us into the shopping precinct. There will be somewhere there,' said Victoria leading them along to the escalator.

Fiona looked at the girls. They were smartly dressed, not at all like the archetypal student. Smart jeans, fashionable Ugg boots, jumper, coat and scarf were a world away from the scruffy, down-at-heel image of students. She followed them up the next escalator to the shopping centre, and found a small café where they could have a quick drink before embarking on their day. As they sat there Fiona wondered how and when it would be best to bring them up to date with recent developments. She did not want to spoil the day that they had been looking forward to, so she suggested shopping, then lunch, followed by a visit to their halls, aiming to catch the train home at about four o'clock, so that Michael could collect her after the shop had shut. This arrangement seemed to suit them both and Fiona asked where they would like to go first. It was a silly question really, thought Fiona, where else but clothes shops, shoe shops, then more clothes shops.

They crossed the road to the Bull Ring, heading for SelfridgesThe amount, and the quality of the goods on display were so different from Fiona's own experience, but the girls seemed very at home there as they wandered through the different departments. Leaving SelfridgesVictoria, who seemed to be the leader, took them on a tour of a remarkable number of clothes outlets, large and small. Fiona could not imagine anyone wearing some of the garments they looked at, but as a middle-aged woman from a small provincial town she was probably out of touch. They then moved on to shoe shops, selling shoes ranging from sensible walking shoes to five inch stilettos. Grace took a fancy to some bright green lookalike sandals, but even priced at £69 they were still a little pricey. Looking forward to the summer Victoria had seen a pair of smart pleated soft shorts, priced at £79. Fiona thought these prices were ridiculous, but on second thoughts she decided to treat Grace to the shoes, and Victoria to the shorts. This afternoon was going to be difficult.

They continued their trawl around the shops of Birmingham city centre until it was lunch time. In addition to the shorts and shoes they had made one or two other purchases, and Fiona had bought a new blouse with the spring and summer in mind. Grace told Fiona that there was a train from New Street to the university campus, and before catching it they had a bite to eat at a tea shop and patisserie in the Bull Ring shopping centre. Putting their shopping bags down carefully at the side of the table, they ordered and awaited their meal. Fiona decided that now was the time to broach the subject she had really come to Birmingham to talk about.

'Remember those folders I gave you at Christmas?' she asked, 'well, I've been doing some more digging and I've come up with some more information to add to them. It is a bit complicated so it might be better if we go back to the university and I can go through it all then. Did you like them?'

'Yes, I did,' said Victoria, 'I think we both did.'

'Yes, that's right. We seem to know so little about Mummy. Oh, sorry, I didn't mean that,' said Grace.

'Don't worry, that's ok, I understand.'

Fiona knew exactly what Grace and Victoria meant. When it came down to it, they were not her daughters. She had adopted them formally after she and Michael were married, but it still wasn't the same, and she did not pretend that it was. Never having had children Fiona was unable to make a direct comparison, but she had seen other women with their children and she realised that she could not replicate that special bond between mother and baby. That was one of the puzzles that concerned her about Deborah and Grace.

Lunch arrived and they ate hungrily. Shopping was hard work. They dropped the subject of mothers and Victoria told Fiona of a fellow student whom she had become friendly with recently. His name was Andrew Boulton, and he was a Politics student. They had met at the Student Union and although Politics and Medieval English were poles apart, they found sufficient in common to spend time together that day, and subsequently. Grace gave Fiona a knowing look, suggesting that Victoria was keener than she was letting on. Victoria, however, was trying to play it cool, but not being very successful. Andrew, or Andy as Victoria called him, was a keen sportsman, and

Victoria had developed a sudden interest in rugby and fencing, two sports in which he excelled. Fiona smiled to herself, enjoying Victoria's slightly embarrassed, yet enjoyable, description of what they did together. Grace had no such romantic attachments; she was too involved in her work, but she was popular with her fellow students, and there was one student, called Perceval, whose name was mentioned more than once. Fiona had difficulty not laughing at the name, but she knew that would have been unforgivable.

Fiona paid the bill and the three women walked down the escalator and stairs to the platform for the train to the university. A few minutes later the train arrived and they all got in. There was no room to sit, but the train soon arrived at their destination and they clambered out, clutching their shopping bags, and Fiona hanging on to her briefcase and handbag. Walking across to the halls Grace said:

'I am looking forward to what you've got to tell us. I think it's been such a good idea doing this for us.'

Fiona smiled weakly, thinking that in an hour or two she might not hold the same opinion. Victoria and Grace both lived on the third floor, and with all their parcels they took the lift. Grace suggested that they used her room as hers was always tidier than Victoria's, which Victoria agreed. They put their parcels down, took off their coats, and settling at the small table Fiona opened her briefcase, in which she had brought the various certificates.

'Victoria,' said Fiona, 'and Grace. Before I explain what I've brought here today I want you to understand that these discoveries make no difference to the way that I feel about you. I shall always love you as my own, nothing can change that. I've made some surprising discoveries, but I've also got unanswered questions still outstanding, so when I explain it all to you I may not have an answer to everything you raise. What I propose to do is to tell you the story I have uncovered, and then you can ask me anything you want to, but as I have said, I won't necessarily have the answers now, but I hope to one day.'

'When you rang up at the beginning of last term for your birth certificates it set off a train of events which have led to where we are now. I'd previously found out that on twins' birth certificates the times of birth are always given so that the older twin can be identified. This can be important in legal matters sometimes. I noticed that on your birth certificates there were no times registered, and I wondered why.'

'What did Dad say? Did you ask him?' enquired Victoria.

'Yes, I did. He said he couldn't remember why that was, he thought the registrar might have just forgotten. Anyway I didn't think any more about it until I noticed that on the certificate, while all your details are the same, apart from the name of course, the births were registered on different days, and recorded by different registrars. Now this is where I don't have an answer, because it would seem that your father wanted to pretend that you were twins, when you weren't.'

Grace and Victoria looked at each other in shocked silence.

'It seems...' continued Fiona, '...as if you must have had different mothers, but the same father, and that something happened to the mother of one of you, and your father wanted to keep you together, so he pretended you were twins. At present I'm not sure which of you is Louise's daughter, but I am still hoping to find that out. I think, but I've not proved this, that Victoria is Louise's daughter. I am only saying this because of your appearance, Victoria;

Louise was tall, slim and fair, but then so is your Dad. I'm not sure of the name of the mother of the other daughter, but I think it might be Deborah. Your father was married to a Deborah Roberts, before he was married to Louise.'

'What does Dad say about all this?' asked the girls together.

'He must know the answer. I'll ring him now and ask him,' said Grace.

'No, please don't just yet.'

Fiona was fumbling for her next word. She took the birth certificates out of her case and showed them to the girls.

'Here you are, you look at this, and I'll put the kettle on. Where are your mugs, Grace?'

'Bottom cupboard, just there,' she said pointing to the cupboard alongside the sink unit.

'I still think we should speak to Dad, or maybe you should, Mum,' said Victoria.

'I shall do when I have everything sorted out. I want to know the full story first, and I still have some gaps. When I have filled those I shall speak to him, but I want to be sure of my facts first. Grace and Victoria pored over the red and cream pieces of paper which had caused so many questions to be asked.

'Well, you're our mother now,' said Grace, supportively.

Victoria was quieter, thinking to herself. If we are not twins but only half-sisters, then there is a woman out there somewhere who is a mother without a child, she thought. Surprisingly Grace appeared to be taking this news better than her sister, as Victoria sat in silence.

'What can you do about this Deborah? Is there anything you can do to prove your theory one way or the other?' said Grace.

'I'm not sure if it will work, but I have advertised on a social networking site for family historians, asking if anyone knows anything about a Deborah Downing or a Deborah Roberts. I haven't had any answer yet.'

'Maybe she's dead,' interrupted Victoria, gloomily.

'She isn't listed on the death indices which go up to 2005,' said Fiona, so, unless she died very recently, it doesn't look as if she is. Until I receive an answer from my advert there is not much more I can do. If I never receive an answer then it may be best just to let matters rest as they are, and not speak to your Dad. Sometimes I wish I hadn't started this quest in the first place.'

Grace put her arms around Fiona.

'Don't be silly, Mum. You were doing it for

us, and it was a very thoughtful thing to do. We were both pleased with it. It's not your fault that these things have come out. Let's be positive and hope that we can find Deborah, and then we can have a lovely family reunion.'

Fiona smiled through her tears at Grace's naivety. If only, she thought, but she had this horrible feeling that it wasn't going to work out like that.

'I don't like it,' said Victoria. 'What does that make us? Floating free with no real idea of who our parents are, after nineteen years of being sure? It's like having your feet cut off. We were on firm ground this morning and you have just cut it away from underneath us. Why did you have to tell us? You could have just let sleeping dogs lie. What has been gained?'

Victoria turned away from Grace and Fiona, and buried her head in her hands.

'I'm sorry, darling,' said Fiona. 'Once I knew I didn't think it would be fair not to tell you. Anyway at the moment I'm not at all sure what happened. I am hoping for a reply to the advert and with a bit of luck that will fill the gaps I have. I shall let you know as soon as I know anything further. In the meantime I do not want to tell your father, because it might hurt him dragging it all up.'

'You didn't mind hurting us,' snapped Victoria.

'Whatever happened, he already knows. I wanted to make sure you knew as well. I know it is difficult to take in, that's why I came on my own to see you. I hoped I could make you understand what I had done, and why I had done it.'

'I know, I'm sorry,' said Victoria. 'I know you have always tried to do the best for us. It's just difficult. Losing Mummy when we did, then all this.

It is as if we are cursed.'

'Don't be silly, Vicky. You don't believe that nonsense. Mum is just trying to do the right thing.'

As they sat around the table they each reflected on a remarkable day. The three women picked up tissues in unison and dried their eyes. They had had an enjoyable day shopping, but it was one shopping trip they would remember forever.

'Anyway, before I go, are you going to try on your clothes and let me see them?'

Both the girls unwrapped their parcels and Victoria tried on the shorts. Her long slender legs were perfectly suited to the style; I wish I had long legs like that, thought Fiona. Grace tried on the sandals and top she had bought. The sandals were ideal for her dainty feet, the colour of the top matched her eyes, and the cut of the top made the most of her figure. How lucky I am, marvelled Fiona, to have two such lovely daughters.

'You both look lovely,' she said, 'I am sure that Andy and Perceval will say the same.'

Grace blushed slightly at the name, and Victoria gave her a sisterly dig in the ribs.

'Thank you, Mum, these are lovely.' said Grace.

'Yes, thank you.'

'I must be going,' said Fiona, 'or I'll miss my train.'

She put on her coat and picked up the certificates which had been left on the table and put them back in her briefcase.

She kissed both girls and said;

'I'll always love you, whatever. I'll always be here for you.'

Both girls sniffed away a tear as they said their goodbyes.

As Fiona left to catch her train Grace and

Victoria stood arm in arm, still looking the same twins as when she had arrived that morning. Having seen her off, they went back into the room and talked about what might come next. They felt so close to each other, having been brought up as twins all their lives. Someone saying they were not had no effect on their relationship; they were twins at heart, if not in blood, and no one could change that.

Fiona's train back to New Street was prompt, and in no time she was back on the train out of Birmingham heading home for Hopley. She had not admitted as much to the girls but she was worried that she would find something unpleasant about Deborah, and she fretted over how she might deal with that. She had been surprised at how they had taken the news, and realised that she had expected Victoria to be the calm one, and Grace to be the one who might react badly. She had no real reason for thinking this; it was just instinct, and wrong as it turned out.

With her head whirling with the day's events Fiona did not fall asleep on the train. She considered what she had said to the girls and whether she could have phrased it differently, but she could not see how. She was still of the opinion that she had to tell them, and she felt she had let them down as gently as could be. She had deliberately not gone into the marriages of Deborah and Louise; that could wait for another day. As for the death or deaths of both women, she thought that best left until there was a definitive answer on Deborah, and for that, she needed a reply to the advert. The train pulled into Hopley station six minutes late, and Fiona could see Michael waiting on the platform. She gathered her possessions together and got off. As she did so Michael greeted her with a brief "hello" and the briefest of pecks on the cheek.

'How are the girls?'

'Fine,' she replied. 'Victoria has found herself a boyfriend - Andy, bit of a sportsman, reading Politics. And Grace has an admirer she is a bit embarrassed about, but I think that might be just his name.'

'What's that then - Asterix?'

'No, now you're being silly; Perceval.'

'Good manly name,' said Michael. 'One of King Arthur's knights. Did you know he was one of only three knights to find the Holy Grail?'

'Go on then, tell me who the others were. I know you are dying to.'

'Sir Galahad and Sir Bors.'

'Well done Mastermind, now can we go home?'

Fiona and Michael walked out of the station to the car and Fiona piled her bags into the boot.

'Did you buy anything?'

'Nothing much, one or two bits and pieces. The girls bought some nice things though.'

Fiona offered no more about the day, and Michael did not ask. They returned home in an uncomfortable silence.

Tim and Madeleine were disappointed that there was no response to the enquiry they had placed on the Internet for news of Deborah, and they were coming to the conclusion that she did not want to be found for some reason. Tim had made the arrangements regarding his part time working and he was looking forward to a change in his lifestyle. He was not a great newspaper reader, but Madeleine, with her background as a vicar's wife, liked to keep up to date with what was going on in the locality. She was briefly looking again through an already-read copy of the prior to putting it with the others papers for recycling, when her eye was caught by a short letter tucked down at the bottom of the page.

'Tim,' she said, excitedly. 'Look at this.'

She pointed to Fiona's letter requesting information about Deborah.

'How very strange,' she said, 'what a

coincidence.'

Tim grabbed the paper from her hand and read the letter.

'This is it!' he exclaimed, 'I'll write straight away.'

'No Tim,' cautioned Madeleine, 'look at the name.'

'Fiona Lewis. Who's she?' replied Tim.

'Just think.' said Madeleine. 'Who is she? She is Michael Downing's third wife. Remember when we were looking for his marriage to Louise? Now why would she be asking for details about Deborah Downing, and why would she be using her maiden name?'

'I don't know,' said Tim, 'only one way to find out, I'll write to her. Don't worry, I'll be careful. I won't tell her that I know she is, or was maybe, Michael's wife. And I won't say anything about my relationship with Deborah. Low key, that's the strategy.'

Tim sat down and drafted out the letter to both their satisfaction and put it ready to post the following day. They both sat back sure that they were on the verge of solving the puzzle of Deborah.

Like Tim Fiona continued to check regularly the website on which she had placed the advert for a contact for Deborah. There was nothing, and she also was becoming disheartened with the whole process. She felt she had found out as much as she could without talking to Michael, and if there continued to be no response she would have to decide whether to let the whole matter drop, or risk what could be a confrontation with Michael. Her letter to the local newspaper had also proved fruitless. She was enjoying her regular morning chat with Paula when she heard the postman at the door of the flat. She went to the post-box by the door, and saw a white envelope on the floor. Picking it up she did not recognise the writing, but what was exciting was that it was addressed to Ms Fiona Lewis. She rushed back into the kitchen

'Paula! Look! It must be about Deborah!'

'Calm down, Fi, open it up, see who it's from.

Might be just some crank.'

Fiona opened the envelope with shaking hands and unfolded the letter. She read it out loud.

Dear Ms Lewis,

EmbertonEcho

Yours sincerely

'What do you think of that? Who is this man?

And why does he want to find Deborah?' said Fiona.

'Questions, questions. Why don't you write

back or ring him. Then you'll find the answer.'

Fiona looked at the letter, uncertain what to do. She would have loved to know who this Tim Lock was, but she was unsure of the next step.

'He might be some nutter. A stalker who's lost touch and finally has found a way to reconnect with his prey,' she said.

'Not after nearly twenty years, surely. He would have found someone else to pester by now. No, I think he's genuine. Why don't you ring him and ask him one or two general questions, and then, if he gives the right answers, offer to meet him somewhere. But it must be somewhere public, a café or pub perhaps, and I would come along.'

'What, as my bodyguard? I like it!' Fiona replied.

'Fi, you've been waiting for months for this

opportunity. You can't let it go now. Get on the phone and see what he has to say. Dial 141 before the number, so that if he is a nutter then he won't have your number.'

'Ok, ok. I will,' agreed Fiona.

She picked up the handset and dialled the number on the letter. It rang and rang. As she was about to put the phone down, it was answered.

'Good morning, Madeleine Porter speaking, how can I help?'

Fiona was thrown by this. She had been expecting a male voice, or at least a female one with the same name as Tim.

'I'm sorry. I think I must have the wrong number. Is that Emberton 693875?'

'Yes, it is. My name is Madeleine Porter. Who were you hoping to speak to?'

The voice was very friendly. An older woman, Fiona guessed. She decided to risk all.

'I was trying to contact Tim Lock, and I was given this number. My name is Fiona Down...Lewis.'

She stumbled over the name as she realised that if it were the right number she would be expected to be Fiona Lewis.

'Yes, of course,' replied Madeleine. 'You are the person Tim wrote to about Deborah, aren't you? Tim's my brother and we live together. My husband died a couple of years ago, that's why we have different names.'

Fiona relaxed. It was the right number after all. Madeleine told her that Tim was at work, but he would love to hear from her. She did not go into details about what she and Tim knew about Deborah, and neither did Fiona.

'What I was hoping to do was to arrange to

meet Mr Lock to share our information about Deborah Downing. I suspect I know things that he doesn't, and I am hoping that the reverse is also true. Do you think he would like to do that?'

'I am sure he would. Why don't we fix a date and I will ask Tim, please call him Tim, to email you and confirm. He works Monday to Friday, so Saturday and Sunday are his only free days. What about Saturday next week?'

'Yes, that would suit me fine,' replied Fiona. 'We could have some lunch in the town and have a chat. Will you come? I had thought about asking a friend of mind, Paula, to join us. My husband works in the bookshop on Saturdays.'

'Yes, I'd love that, but I am busy on Saturdays usually. Let me know your email and I will speak to Tim when he comes home from work. He'll contact you then. Do you know, it is so odd that you put that letter in the because Tim had put an advert on the Internet, trying to find someone who knew Deborah. All will become clear, I am sure, when you meet up with Tim. Thanks so much for calling. Goodbye.'

Fiona was so excited. She told Paula what Madeleine had said, and they both agreed that they would tell Michael that they were going out for the day on that Saturday.

Later that evening Fiona checked her email and there was a message from Tim Lock, expressing his pleasure at being contacted, and fixing the meeting for Saturday week at the WaggonandHorsesin Hopley, at 12.30pm. He gave Fiona a brief description of himself so that she would recognise him, and Fiona did the same. Fiona's life continued almost on autopilot from then until the following Saturday. She was like a girl looking forward to a first date. Michael would wonder what was going on, she thought, but he didn't notice. He didn't notice very much these days.

Fiona prepared early for her meeting with Tim. She carefully collected all her certificates that she had acquired over the weeks and put them in her briefcase. She dressed smartly and made a special effort with her hair. She wanted to create a good impression with Tim, and with Paula there he would not think she was trying to seduce him. She left Michael busy in the shop and told him she was going over to Paula's for the day. Arriving at her house just after eleven o'clock there was plenty of time to plan tactics. Fiona had only spoken to Madeleine, although she had had the friendly email, but she was still apprehensive about meeting this man face-to-face. Paula complimented her on her appearance, saying she looked dressed to kill, and Fiona explained that was not the intention but she did not want to appear to be some scruffy ne'er-do-well.

They agreed that Fiona would introduce herself as Fiona Lewis, but then explain that she was married to Michael Downing, but she was using her maiden name for this purpose. The plan then was to let Tim do the talking and find out exactly how much he did know, and how much, as they had always thought about Sam Wainwright, he was just guessing.

Fiona was feeling the butterflies as they got back into her car and drove into town to the WaggonandHorses, where she parked in the car park behind the pub. It was approaching twenty past twelve and as they got out of the car they saw a man in his fifties, stocky with greying hair, walking into the bar.

'That's him,' cried Paula excitedly.

'Maybe,' cautioned Fiona. 'Let's get inside and see.'

'They walked into the bar and there he was, where they had arranged, sitting by the bar, looking nervous.

'Tim Lock?' enquired Fiona. 'My name's Fiona Lewis.'

The man turned round. His dark eyes met Fiona's gaze and he smiled.

'Hello, good to see you. I thought I saw you as I came into the bar. And you are Paula, I presume?'

He held out his hand in greeting and Paula shook it.

'Yes, I am. I hope you don't mind me coming. Fiona and I thought it better to meet together in a public place first. I know that sounds awful, but it's sensible don't you think?'

Paula could hear herself gabbling on. She always did when she was nervous, although there was no reason for her to be so.

'No, of course not. I had hoped my sister Madeleine was going to be able to come, but she is busy today with something she could not put off.'

Fiona walked up to the bar and ordered some drinks.

'What would you like, Tim?'

'Pint, bitter, please.'

She ordered a fruit juice for her and Paula, and waited for Tim's pint. Then she carried the tray on which the barman had put the drinks across to a quiet corner of the bar, where she hoped they would not be disturbed. As she had invited Tim to come to her, Fiona thought she should speak first.

'Tim, I'm so glad you could come. There's so much to talk about, but I wanted to make one thing clear at the outset. I am married to Michael Downing, and I only used my maiden name on this occasion because I did not want it to prevent any contact being made. My husband does not know that I am meeting you; he is not keen on my pursuing these enquiries. Michael and I married in 1997, after his previous wife was killed in a car crash. I started to build the family tree for my daughters, Grace and Victoria, when they went away to university last September. That is what has brought me to this situation now.'

Tim nearly spilled his beer.

'Your daughter Grace?' he spluttered.

'Yes,' replied Fiona. 'To be accurate, they are both my adopted daughters. I adopted them after Michael and I were married.'

'I'm sure this will come as a shock to you, but I believe Grace is my daughter.'

This time it was Fiona's turn to be taken aback.

'I'm sorry,' she said, 'I just need a minute. Excuse me.'

Fiona stood up and turned away from Tim and headed for the ladies'. Paula followed her, concerned. Fiona went in and stood with her hands on one of the basins, looking in the mirror. Tears formed in her eyes and started to run down her cheeks, ruining her mascara and make-up. Paula put her arm around her shoulder.

'His daughter! What's all this about? What have I done?' Fiona cried. 'Digging up all this, for nothing. What am I going to tell those girls now? It was difficult enough before.'

She pulled a tissue out of her bag and started to dry her eyes, smearing her make-up even more.

'What a sight I must look now.'

'Don't worry about that,' consoled Paula, 'What do you think of this chap and his story?'

'Well, we haven't heard his story yet, have we? Could he be Grace's father? It's possible, I suppose, but proving it could be rather difficult.'

'Fix your make-up and let's go and see what he has to say for himself,' suggested Paula, 'but I don't think we should do anything too drastic at the moment.

We'll hear what he has to say and then tell him we want to consider what to do next.'

'OK. Thanks Paula, you are always so sensible. I don't know what I would do without you.'

Fiona opened her bag and took out her make-up and looked in the mirror again.

Back in the pub Tim sat and stared at the door leading to the ladies'. He wished he hadn't said what he had said quite so bluntly. He hadn't intended it that way, but when Fiona had said about daughter it had just slipped out. Madeleine would not be happy with him when he got home, and he sat wondering what he should do next.

The pub was busy and although they were in the corner of the bar Tim was wondering if it was really the best place for such private discussions. Just as he was doing so he saw Fiona and Paula returning to the table.

'I'm so sorry,' apologised Fiona. 'It was such a shock to hear you say what you did about Grace. I really am not sure that here is the best place for this conversation. Why don't we have some lunch and then go somewhere else?'

'Just what I was thinking' replied Tim.

'There's a small room at the back of the pub.' said Paula. 'Why don't we order some lunch and ask them to serve it there. It would be more private. Let's have a look at the menu.'

All three of them picked up a menu and perused the enticing range of dishes on offer. Having chosen, Paula asked that they serve the lunch in the back room, which they agreed. They also ordered soft drinks as they were driving, and then they moved into the other room and awaited the arrival of the meals, which were not long in coming. Tim's revelation about

Grace was put to one side while they ate, and over lunch Tim told them about his job and his plans to go part-time, and Fiona was very interested in his allotment idea. Paula thought that there seemed to be an immediate connection between them as she watched Fiona, her eyes fixed on Tim while he was speaking. He was a good-looking man, she thought; Fiona was married, but it had never stopped people in the past. Tim's gaze was also reserved for Fiona, her slim figure shown off in her smart jacket and skirt, and her hair done to perfection, even after the upset earlier. Paula thought she could detect a faint whiff of Chanel, and she knew it was not her, and it was certainly not Tim.

Lunch over, they ordered coffee and tea, and returned to business.

'Before we go any further' said Fiona, 'I want to make it clear that at the moment I would just like to hear the full story and then consider what we do next. I don't want to rush into something I may regret later.

And certainly I do not want to confront Michael with any of this information today. We can always meet again if necessary.'

'I'm ok with that,' agreed Tim.

'So if Michael Downing is their father and Fiona adopted both the girls, How are you their father?' interrupted Paula, puzzled.

'Not father,' corrected Tim, 'Grace's father. I don't know about Victoria.'

'But I have their birth certificates here,' said Fiona, reaching down to her case.

'May I have a look at those?' asked Tim. 'I have been trying to get copies but I didn't have all the information I required.'

'Yes, of course,' said Fiona as she handed the certificates over the table.

Tim looked at them and a scowl crossed his face as he read them.

'What is going on? Grace's birthday is 11 March and this says it was 5 March. Why has Michael done that?'

'Sorry, I can't tell you,' replied Fiona. 'As far as I knew, Grace's and Victoria's birthdays were the 5 March. Why do you say it is the 11?'

'Never mind for the moment,' replied Tim. 'Let me tell you my side of this story, and it may become clear. Then you can tell me afterwards what you know that I don't, and between us we should be able to build a complete picture. After all, my purpose in coming here is to trace Deborah's whereabouts.'

'OK, fire away.'

Fiona and Paula settled back in their seats and gave Tim the floor.

'I have never been married,' he started, 'but over the years I have had a number of girlfriends, lady friends if you like, there's no proper word is there? Anyway I met Deborah Downing in about 1991 through work. We both worked at Emberton Borough Council as it was in those days. I knew she was married, but we just hit it off. Deborah told me how her husband was a spendthrift, a waster and how uncaring he was. It is difficult to explain why but we fell in love, even though she was married. He was away a lot, at the local athletics club, and we saw each other frequently. In the autumn of 1992 she told me that she was pregnant. She was convinced that the child was mine as we had been seeing a lot of each other. She did, however, say that there was a very slim chance that the baby was Michael's. Their relationship at the time was not good, and she thought he was having an affair with someone at work.'

'Anyway, once she was pregnant, Deborah and

I saw less of each other. Michael became very protective of her, wanted her to have the baby at home and he stopped going out so much. He also persuaded her to give up work early in the pregnancy. As a result of all this Deborah and I couldn't have much contact.

When the baby was finally born, she telephoned me and said she knew the baby was mine, said she looked like me, and that she was going to call her Grace. At no time did she mention a baby named Victoria. All the time during the pregnancy I had been trying to persuade her to leave Michael, come to me, and start divorce proceedings. Shortly after the birth I tried to telephone her, but the calls were unanswered. Then I tried writing to her but the letters were returned "gone away". I assumed from this that for some reason she had decided to stay with Michael, and I stopped any attempt at further contact. I loved Deborah very much and I must say I was very distressed when she seemed to cut me off. Over the years I've got used to it, and until recently I had not given thought to her or Grace for a long time. Then my sister Madeleine got in to this family history business, and it brought it all back. I saw your letter in the andit seemed like fate. There are a couple of odd things that have come out of what you have just shown me. You know I said to you that Deborah telephoned me when Grace was born; well she phoned on 11 March. I can't forget that date; the date that my only child was born. Yet on her birth certificate Michael Downing has put her birth as 5 March. Very strange. But even stranger is that her mother has been registered as Louise not Deborah. I don't understand it. So what I would like is to meet up with Deborah again, and also meet my daughter for the first time.'

Tim stopped and took a long swallow of his drink. His eyes were a little misty, but he fought to keep himself together. He leaned back in his seat and looked at the two women facing him. He realised that he might have just destroyed Fiona's faith in her husband, but he had a suspicion that she was not entirely surprised with his revelations. Fiona and Paula sat quietly. It was a lot to take in all in one go. This means, thought Fiona, that not only are the girls not twins, they are not even sisters. It had been difficult enough when she had been to see them recently; this could make things even worse. She pondered how to deal with it, but as Tim had been so honest with his story, it was only fair that she should be also. It would probably be as shocking to Tim as his story had been to her.

She took up the story.

'I met Michael when I was a customer in the bookshop back in the mid-nineties. At that time he was married to Louise, and had two little girls, whom I babysat. Louise died in a terrible car crash when a lorry drove into her car head on, and she was killed outright. I knew the girls well, and Michael and I were very fond of each other. We married not long afterwards and it all worked out well. When the twins went off to university last autumn I started to do a bit of family history research for them, so they could learn a bit more about their mother, whom they could barely remember. Before all this I knew nothing about Michael having been married before Louise, and I thought that the girls were Louise's children. I then discovered that the birth of the twins, for that's what they appeared to be and what Michael had always said they were, was before he and Louise were married. He said that she was pregnant before they married and they didn't have time to get married with him losing his job and moving house. I had no reason to disbelieve this until I found during my research that Michael had been married to a Deborah Roberts back in 1987. Having made that discovery, coupled with the information on the birth certificates, it seemed obvious that he had a pregnant wife and a pregnant lover at the same time, and that he was the father of both babies. This does not now seem to be the case.'

'The big mystery seems to be Deborah,' said Paula. 'If Michael registered both babies as Louise's, passing them off as twins, why didn't Deborah stop him? Tim, do you have any ideas?'

'I don't know. I must say that when I was coming here I thought that you would be able to put me in touch with Deborah, at least. Now, it seems, you know no more than I do. I know about Deborah's life with Michael before Louise, and you, Fiona, know about Louise's life with Michael before you married him. The two girls don't appear to be even sisters, if I am the father of Grace and Deborah the mother, and Michael is the father of Victoria and Louise the mother. Where does all that get us? I would like to meet Grace, certainly, but I know that can't happen this visit. The only person who knows the answer to this conundrum is Michael. I know what you said earlier, but don't you think that we ought to speak to him?"

Fiona looked very uncertain.

'I'm not sure,' she said. 'He knows that I have been doing some family research, and he knows that I have discovered that the girls were born before he married Louise. I also raised with him the question of the lack of times on the birth certificates if the girls were twins. When twins are born, Tim, the times of birth are recorded, but they were not for Grace and Victoria. He has just pretended that they were twins all these years to cover up the true parentage of Grace. As I said earlier I would like time just to absorb everything you have told me. Nobody is going anywhere and we can always talk again. I really don't want to do any more today. I'm sorry, Tim, if you feel you have had an unnecessary journey here, but I think that would be for the best. What I will do, though, is to copy and email to you all the documents we have been looking at today; then you will have everything together.

'Thanks. That would be useful. Madeleine

and I have talked about all this and we did wonder whether Michael was covering up Grace's parentage, although of course, we did not know how, or even why. I think that we are going to have to ask him if we want to know the answers. Between us we have done all we can to solve the mystery. But I think you're right, we can always leave that for another day, but I don't want to leave it too long. We have enough to think about for the time being, and I would like to talk to Madeleine and get her view before going any further. Anyway it would be nice to come up and see you again.'

Tim finished his drink and stood up. He smiled and held out his hand to Fiona.

Fiona took his hand and held it, just a little longer than necessary perhaps, as she stood up. She smiled back at him.

'It's been very helpful meeting you, Tim. Thanks for taking the trouble to come. We will meet again when we can sort this out once and for all. Take care driving home and do stay in touch.'

The bill paid, Paula and Fiona walked out towards the car, leaving Tim at the door of the pub waving. As they got into their car they could see him crossing the car park to his own car.

'He's rather nice,' said Paula. 'Took a bit of a shine to you. Mind you. I don't think it was all one way. You've only just met him Fi. I'm shocked!'

Fiona gently blushed and changed the subject.

'Never mind about that, what do you think about what he said? Could he be Grace's father? He seemed very sure.'

'Let's get home. It's too much to take in all at once. Sleep on it and think again. Then you can ask him to come again. You'll like that,' she teased.

Paula dropped her friend off at the bookshop,

and Fiona went round the back to go in to the flat rather than through the shop. She didn't feel she could face Michael after the lunch conversation at the pub. As she walked in she could hear Michael's voice in the shop, chatting to customers in that friendly, easy way which had been his hallmark over the years she had known him. Could he really be the bigamous adulterer that her research appeared to be showing him to be? There must be another answer, but she could not work out what it could be.

She sat in 'Paula's' chair and closed her eyes, gently dozing. As she was drifting off to sleep she remembered his distress at Louise's accident, his love and care for the twins, both when little and whilst growing up, and his love for her over fourteen years. Was all that a fake? Surely not. But could anyone have those feelings and still have done what he seems to have done? It was all very puzzling. She was enjoying her half-sleep when she was woken with a start by the birdsong-like noise of the phone. She jumped up, anxious to get to the phone before Michael came through from the shop.

'Hello. Oh, hello Paula. Sorry I was just nodding, thinking over things...No, I really can't believe it all... Michael's not like that. Thanks for today, anyway. Yes, plenty of food for thought. See you Tuesday, as usual. 'Bye.'

Tim was eager to get home to tell Madeleine what he had learned. Arriving home just after six o'clock Madeleine was waiting for him. She had been hoping he would have rung during the day to bring her up to date with developments, but he had not, and she was now very anxiously waiting for news.

'Come on then. Tell all. Food will have to wait until I know what's been going on.'

Tim shrugged off his coat, took his shoes off and settled in his favourite chair. After a few moments thought he told Madeleine the full story, not forgetting to elaborate on the attractive Mrs Fiona Downing.

'Tim!' exclaimed Madeleine.

'Sorry, but she was very friendly, and also rather troubled in her exploration of Michael's history. We did say we would meet again, but I said I wanted to talk to you first. What do you think?'

'I think putting your two stories together you have got to the stage of there being only two possible answers. One is that Deborah did leave home shortly after the birth for some reason, and hasn't wanted to be found over these last twenty years. Or she's dead, either accidently or deliberately.'

Tim was alarmed at this suggestion as, surprisingly, he had not considered the possibility of death as an answer.

What was it Fiona had said? He mused. She and Michael were fond of each other? Was that before

Louise's death in this car accident? Had Michael tired of Deborah, killed her, then tired of Louise when Fiona came on the scene and killed her too? Fiona was an attractive woman; I could see why Michael might have been drawn to her. No, surely not; but then I haven't met him.

'I was going to say...' continued Madeleine, '...sometimes women have problems after giving birth and it is not completely unknown for them to reject their babies, and in extreme circumstances even kill them. Maybe Deborah just could not face it and decided to leave sooner rather than later. But where would she go, I wonder?'

'If Deborah walked out like that wouldn't Michael want to try to find her?' wondered Tim.

'Not necessarily. Especially if he has a ready-made substitute mother in Louise to take over. But I wonder what he planned to do if Deborah hadn't left?

Maybe Deborah was going to come to you after all.'

Tim was lost in thought again. If only she had come to him, maybe they would have had more children. Tim visualised himself with Deborah, surrounded by a growing family, happy in the love of a good woman. Tears formed in his eyes as he looked on this vision, realising that that was all it was.

'Tim, you've gone again. Listen, I have an idea. Before we go any further and challenge Michael on what happened we need to check every possibility. The records office keeps back copies of local newspapers, and if they don't have them they may still be available from the newspaper itself. We should check for any reports of missing persons or accidents in the paper around the time of Deborah's disappearance. Even if she left Michael she might have come to grief in an accident, and as he moved away very shortly after her leaving he might have never known. That would certainly explain why she never contacted you, or tried to see her baby again.'

'Well it's a better scenario than the one I was thinking about a moment ago,' said Tim.

'I'll go into town next week and do some more digging,' said Madeleine. 'Now, let's have something to eat and change the subject.'

They both went through to the kitchen to prepare some food, but Tim could not put out of his mind the thought of him with Deborah and children in their own home.

The weekend dragged by for Fiona. Life with Michael was no longer the same. Prior to this investigation she felt she had a good marriage and a good husband, one she could rely on and trust. Now all that was in the balance. She was constantly trying to match up the Michael Downing she married and had lived with happily and faithfully for fourteen years, with the Michael Downing who was the spendthrift, lying adulterer appearing in her researches. As a result they spent less and less time together. He was more engrossed in his business and she found jobs and work around the house and garden to keep her occupied. He did not realise the extent of her knowledge of his previous life, but he did know that she had discovered some things, and perhaps suspected she had found out others. For her part she was finding it more difficult to be close and loving with all this hanging over her. She was beginning to wish she had never started, and she could have lived the rest of her life in blissful ignorance. Tuesday, and Paula's visit, could not come quickly enough.

The shop was unusually busy for a Tuesday in February and Michael just waved to Paula as she made her way through the shop into the flat.

'Hello, Fi. Nice to be back in our routine.'

She sniffed the rich coffee aroma in the kitchen as she sat down.

'Smells good.'

'Yes, I bought a different brand for you to try. Thought it sounded tasty. Can anything sound tasty?'

'Now, what thoughts have you been having over the weekend?' She asked. 'Mmm, tastes tasty anyway,' she added, sipping her coffee.

Fiona sat thoughtfully. She was finding it difficult to know where to go and what to do next. Until recently she had been happy with Michael, with her life in the bookshop, with the girls, and at work for Unity. It was as if all that was going to come crashing down around her, and there was nothing she could do to stop it.

'I really don't know what to do next,' she replied, 'I've been turning it all over in my mind over the weekend and I am no further forward. Tim's a really nice, genuine chap, and he was clearly hurt by what happened with Grace and Deborah. That's what makes it all so difficult. I am not sure whether I could carry on with Michael now even if we found out nothing more. The last fourteen years have been on false pretences.'

'He has been good to you, though, Fi. He's always been faithful hasn't he? He's provided for you and the girls. And he clearly loves them very much.'

'That could change once he realises he is not Grace's father. Who knows?'

Fiona reached out for the tissues and dabbed her eyes.

'It started out as such a good idea for the girls and look where it has got me. Maybe I'll put a warning on the family history websites. DON'T DO IT!'

She grimaced through her tears.

'Have you spoken to Tim or emailed him?' asked Paula.

'Yes, I sent him copies of all the bits and pieces we looked at on Saturday. But I haven't made any arrangement to meet up again.'

'Why don't you have a word with Madeleine? See what her take on it all is.'

With that the phone beeped in the kitchen and Fiona snatched it up.

'Hello, this is Madeleine Porter. Is Fiona there?'

'Hello Madeleine. This is Fiona. That's funny, my friend Paula and I were just talking about you. She suggested I rang you to find out what your view was on this whole business.'

'Well, Tim's out at work at the moment and if you have a moment we can perhaps share one or two ideas.'

'Yes, that's fine. Michael's busy in the shop so we won't be disturbed.'

'After Tim's visit on Saturday we had a long chat about what he had found out. You must realise that Tim and Deborah were very much in love, and he was delighted when he learned about the baby. Then he was very cut up when she disappeared and he didn't see her. As the years went by he talked about Deborah less and less, and then last week he saw your letter in the he was so excited. Obviously after the weekend he was very keen to speak to Michael and find out everything, but I advised against this until we had exhausted every avenue of investigation. As a result, I went into town yesterday and searched back copies of the local newspaper. I wanted to see if there was any mention of a Deborah Downing or Deborah Roberts being involved in an accident around the time of her disappearance. I also looked to see if there was any missing person reported at that time. Sadly I found absolutely nothing. No missing persons, no accidents, no mysterious happenings. It's as if she disappeared off the face of the earth.'

'I suppose if Michael was happy with Louise then he wouldn't report her as missing. What about family and friends. Wouldn't they have missed her?'

'Tim said once that Deborah's parents were both dead and that she was an only child. I think she had friends at work, but after she left to have the baby maybe they lost touch. Tim never met any of her friends, but then I suppose he wouldn't have done.'

Fiona's heart sank at this news. She kept hoping there was going to be an explanation that didn't include death, but this was now looking less likely.

'No, I suppose not,' replied Fiona. 'It seems to me that all that is left is to speak to Michael and find out his version of events. What is Tim doing this coming Saturday? Maybe he could come up again and we could have a further chat and then speak to Michael?'

'As I said he's at work at the moment but I'm sure he would like that. I'll get him to email you tonight just to confirm. Meet in the pub again?'

'Yes. I'll look forward to it.'

Madeleine rang off and Fiona looked across at Paula, who was frowning.

'There's no choice, is there?' said Fiona, 'either

we talk to Michael or drop the whole thing. 'But Tim is going to want to speak to him anyway. He wants to know what happened to the mother of his child, and to meet his now grown-up baby

Paula did not come to the pub on Saturday. She was not sure that she wanted to continue this investigation and thought that any subsequent conversation between Fiona and Michael, with or without Tim, was going to be too intimate to involve her. As she had done previously Fiona dressed smartly for the occasion and was greeted in the car park with a peck on the cheek from Tim.

'You look nice,' he smiled.

'Thanks. Hello again.'

Fiona and Tim went into the bar and ordered a drink and sat down with the menu. Fiona was distracted, thinking about Michael and what might happen in the afternoon. They ordered their meal but Fiona was unable to enjoy the food. Tim, on the other hand, seemed unconcerned and was eating heartily. Upon finishing their meal Tim stood up and went across to the bar to pay leaving Fiona sitting, deep in thought.

'Right, let's go and see Michael and sort this out,' he said, returning to the table.

'Just a minute Tim, I think I need a breath of fresh air first.'

Fiona stood up, put on her coat and walked towards the door. The February wind was cold, although the sun shone weakly through the afternoon clouds.

'This way,' she beckoned to Tim, walking out and through the car park. 'We'll come back for the car.'

She headed along the street leading out of the town, Tim struggling to catch up with her.

'Hold on. Where are we going?'

'There's a walk through the old part of the town that starts along here. It cuts through the houses and old shops and comes back down to the High Street. It's not far but it gives me the chance to prepare myself.'

Tim nodded and walked alongside her, tempted to take her hand in his, but he realised that Fiona was well known in the town and it would look odd if she were seen walking hand in hand with another man. He satisfied himself with the private pleasure of being in her company and walking with her.

The walk took longer than Tim had anticipated, as they made various stops along the way, but eventually they returned to the High Street. Fiona pointed out the bookshop and explained that the flat had a rear entrance. They walked round to the back and went in.

Saturday afternoons were not the bookshop's busiest time. Michael had expected that it would be when he first took the shop over, but during the years he had run it business had been at best patchy. Major sporting events took their toll, as did other local activities, always vying for potential shoppers' attention on a Saturday. Late February afternoons could be especially slow, and the day that Fiona came in with Tim was no exception.

Fiona and Tim had come into the kitchen and Fiona invited him to take a seat while she made a drink. Following on from their conversation in the pub she thought it would be a good idea to show Tim some photographs of Grace, so while he was drinking his tea she went upstairs to find some of their photograph albums. She came downstairs carrying three, containing photographs of Grace at different ages. When she showed him the pictures of her as a baby he was very moved, and Fiona put her hand on his shoulder to console him. He looked back up at her and smiled, and she could see Grace's eyes in his. He continued to look through the albums, stopping every so often to examine particular photographs more closely. She squeezed his shoulder and he put his hand on hers.

Suddenly there was a call from Michael as he came through from the shop. Fiona jumped away from Tim guiltily, as he opened the kitchen door. Michael stopped, looked confused, and said:

'Fiona, has the electricity gone off out here? The lights have gone off in the shop and the computer has gone down. Who's this?'

'Michael, this is Tim, he has been doing family research as I have, and we seem to have some relatives in common. I was just showing him some pictures of Grace.'

She moved over towards the light switch and turned it on. The light came on as normal,

'Seems OK here. Go back into the shop and

try again.'

Michael did so and the electricity was working. The computer beeped as it rebooted itself, and the lights returned.

'OK here now,' he called.

Fiona blushed as she looked back towards Tim.

'Sorry, I shouldn't have done that,' she said.

'Done what? Your hand on my shoulder felt nice. Nothing wrong with that.'

Fiona blushed again, this time deeper than before. She had taken her jacket off and left it upstairs when she had fetched the photograph albums, and she was now more than ever aware of Tim's gaze.

'I am a married woman, don't forget,' said Fiona. 'I think that we should call Michael through and tell him why you are really here.'

Fiona was feeling a little guilty as she was

enjoying Tim's attention. It had seemed so long since Michael had behaved in such a way towards her, but in truth it was probably only a matter of weeks. Something though, had been lost, Fiona thought, which could never be refound.

It was just after four o'clock when Fiona called to Michael to ask him to come into the kitchen. As he came through Fiona said to him:

'Michael, there is something very important we need to speak about. I think you should close the shop early.'

Michael was a stickler for times, and he did not like closing the shop when it should be open. He hesitated, and Fiona spoke again, more firmly this time.

'Michael, it really is very important. Please close the shop.'

Michael was worried. He could not understand what there was that was so important that made Fiona insist that he shut up shop. Reluctantly he walked back into the shop, put off the lights, closed the door and locked it. He wrote a brief note which he put on the door explaining that the shop was closed for emergency reasons. He returned to the kitchen and sat down.

'What's so important then? And who is this man?'

'I told you,' Fiona replied, 'Tim has been tracing his family tree like me, and that is why he is here.'

Michael got up to go.

'I'm not closing the shop just for that,' he said.

'It's not just for that,' replied Fiona, impatiently. 'Just sit down and listen.'

'Tim was a friend of Deborah Downing, and he has been trying to trace her as he has not seen her for many years. We got in touch because he answered an advertisement I placed in the asking for anyone who had any information about Deborah to contact me.'

'Deborah Downing?' asked Michael.

'Yes, Michael, you know who she is, or was. Tim and I have pieced together a large part of Deborah's story but we don't know it all. We would like you to tell us. We know, for example, that she is Grace's mother.'

Michael's face fell. Why had he not put a stop to this family tree exploration earlier? It was always going to end here.

'Pour me a cup of that tea, then.'

Michael settled into Paula's chair to start his tale.

'OK, you have found me out. There are some things in this story which I am not especially proud of, but there we are, you will see that as I go along. I met

Deborah Roberts in 1981 when she was working for the council and I was at the library in Emberton. We saw each other on and off, but then got closer and I moved in with her and her mother in 1985. Her mother was seriously ill by this time and I helped Deborah to look after her. In November I think it was, in 1986, Mrs Roberts died, and Deborah and I continued living in the same house. In the June of the following year we got married. After we married Deborah's behaviour towards me changed. We had never had a lot of money, but with the death of her mother Deborah had inherited the house, and also some savings, not a lot. She became very mean with it, checking everything I was spending and telling me off if I didn't consult with her first. In those days I was doing some running and some training at the Emberton Runners, the local athletics club, and I was spending time each week there. I think that Deborah resented my interests that she didn't share, so I was permanently in trouble for that. Added to all this, my parents were very ill, they both had dementia and were in a home. You remember I told you about my brother, Ian, and his refusal to help with the fees for my Mum and Dad? Well, Deborah resented my paying them out of our money.'

Tim looked at Fiona as Michael was talking. He shook his head gently and Fiona remembered his description of Deborah and Michael's relationship; different, to put it mildly.

'All in all, the marriage was not particularly happy. It had been so different before we were married. Anyway we plodded on, but then in the summer of 1990 I met Louise Baxter. She had been a trainee librarian, but had failed her exams, and then she came to work in the library just as an assistant. She was tall, she was slim, and she was beautiful.'

Michael's face changed as soon as he mentioned Louise. His eyes lit up, and he smiled as he pictured her in his mind.

'I was bowled over,' he continued. 'I wanted to see her all the time, and Deborah's nagging at home didn't matter any more, as long as I could look forward to the next time I was going to be with Louise. We started seeing each other regularly. She loved me as passionately as I loved her. It was wonderful. Then one day, one very hot, sultry day in late summer 1992, she told me she was pregnant. I was absolutely over the moon. I remember it as if it were yesterday. She told me over lunch at her house in Edward Street in Emberton, and I remember, after lunch, looking out of the window over the garden, thinking about Deborah, and wondering what would happen.'

Michael's eyes were tearful at this reminiscence. Fiona had poured the tea he had asked for and he turned to take a sip.

'I never stopped loving Louise, but when I arrived home that evening Deborah had some surprising news. She was pregnant as well. I was a somewhat taken aback because we had not been, how shall I put it, over-friendly recently, but there had been one occasion. However, after this she became brighter and more cheerful. So now I had two babies to look forward to. Louise left work quite early in her pregnancy, and I persuaded Deborah to do the same. I wanted the best for Deborah and the baby, so I spent more time at home and less time at the "Runners". My Mum and Dad were getting worse, so I did carry on visiting them regularly, but they knew nothing about the babies. As it turned out both of them died before the girls were born.'

'About six months into the pregnancies I received notice from the library. Town Hall cuts were having their effect, and I had to start looking for another job. I wanted to stay with books, so I identified this small bookshop which was for sale. I persuaded Deborah it was a good idea and, fortunately, we sold the house quickly and committed ourselves to buying the bookshop. Deborah was not keen on the idea of moving away, but with the jobs market as it was then we had no choice, so she agreed, reluctantly.'

So far there was little that Michael had said that both Tim and Fiona did not know. He had admitted to the marriage to Deborah and the relationship with Louise, but nothing major had been revealed. Fiona noted that he said that Grace was his child, so clearly he had not thought of the possibility of a lover. She and Tim were not going to challenge him on that at the moment. As they were sitting at the table, Fiona's hand crept towards Tim's and entwined itself around his fingers. She gave a gentle squeeze and he responded.

'Louise's baby, Victoria, was born on 5 March, and six days later, on 11 March, Grace was born.'

Michael hesitated. Fiona wondered what he was going to say. This was the bit she had been waiting for.

'Then something strange happened,' said

Michael. 'Grace was born on the 11 March, which was a Sunday. As planned she had the baby at home, and it was early in the morning. On the Tuesday morning she walked out of the house and I never saw her again. I searched and searched. I contacted the police and hospitals, all to no avail. I was left with this two-day old infant with no mother. Louise moved in and helped with Grace as well as looking after Victoria. On the previous Friday I had registered Victoria's birth, with Louise as the mother of course. As a result of Deborah walking out like she did I decided to register Grace's birth, with Louise as the mother as well, and bring them up as twins. As you know I lied on the birth certificates about Louise and I being married, so I didn't think it would matter to lie about Grace's birth as well. If it hadn't been for this investigation of yours none of this would have come to light, and everyone would still be happy. I don't know what happened to Deborah, and when the time came for us to move house and take over the business, that all went through because the documents had been signed in advance, and the new bank account opened. Louise came with me to Hopley and we pretended that we were the parents of twin girls. Then one day Louise signed an authorisation form asking the Bank to transfer the account to another bank account just in my name. Banks haven't checked signatures for years, and they transferred the account as requested. Like I said, Deborah just disappeared off the face of the earth, maybe she had some other bloke, and went off with him, or couldn't cope with the baby, who knows?'

Tim and Fiona sat and listened in silence. They were astonished that Michael could fabricate such a story so quickly, or had he been making it up for a long time, just in case this occasion ever arose? They thought there were so many holes in it that it was difficult to believe that Michael really thought anyone would swallow it. Fiona spoke first, trying to contain her anger,

'Michael, that is so obviously a pack of lies. It can't be true for so many reasons. Why was there no record of her as a missing person? Why was there nothing in the newspapers about a young mother going missing and deserting her baby? And what have you to say to the main reason for it being untrue, who is sitting right here,'

Michael looked across at Tim, sitting next to Fiona at the table. Tim said quietly:

'Deborah did have another "bloke" as you say. It was me. And I am Grace's father.'

Michael was stunned. For the whole of Grace's life he had believed he was her father; he had nurtured her, cared for her, watched her grow up into an attractive young woman. Now this stranger had arrived on his doorstep trying to take all this away from him. He sat forward and looked at Fiona,

'What do you know about this? Is it true?' he asked angrily.

'Tim's sister, Madeleine has been tracing her family tree, and when she was doing this it reminded Tim of his relationship with Deborah, and the baby they had. He came here today hoping to track down Deborah, possibly make contact with Grace, and introduce himself to her as her father.'

'And you,' he said, turning to Tim. 'You think you can just march in here and tell me you are my daughter's father. How do you know you are? You can't have taken any test. How can you prove it? When Deborah told me she was pregnant, I was surprised, but it was not impossible. Even if you had been sleeping with her at the same time, it doesn't prove she's your baby.'

'No. it doesn't,' agreed Tim. 'But when Grace was born Deborah rang me and told me. She also said she was 99% certain I was the father. She said that you only had sex with her once that month, and after four childless years I think you being the father is unlikely. Our relationship was, what can I say, more regular than that. I am sure that I am Grace's father, but if you want to take a test, I am very willing to do so.'

Michael slumped back in the chair, apparently beaten. He thought back to those months before she had announced the pregnancy, and remembered how she had changed. He had not considered that it was because she was receiving the love and affection that he should have been giving her, from elsewhere. On reflection that made sense; he had been, after all, too preoccupied with Louise to take much notice. He turned again to Tim.

'So how did you end up coming here? If you had wanted to find Grace you have had nearly twenty years to do it.'

Fiona interrupted.

'That was me; I wrote a letter to the asking if anyone knew anything about Deborah Roberts or Deborah Downing. I wrote the letter because I had found out that you had been married to a Deborah Roberts in Emberton back in 1987, and I could not find out what had happened to her. I thought that perhaps someone from Emberton would know the answer. Tim replied.'

'Thanks for going behind my back,' said Michael sarcastically. 'Just what a dutiful wife should do. Why didn't you come and ask me, I'd have told you all about it.'

'What! Like you just have! That cock and bull story about Deborah walking out and leaving her two-day old baby. Pull the other one, Michael.'

Michael stood up and walked towards Fiona, towering over her,

'You bitch! Get out!'

Fiona had never seen Michael like this. He was not a man to lose his temper, not in her experience anyway, but now he had totally lost control. Tim got up out of the chair and pushed the Michael away.

'Sit down and listen!' Tim said.

Michael was not going to be treated like that in his own house, and as he steadied himself he grabbed hold of a knife from the block on the work surface, and waved it threateningly at Tim.

Paula had not wanted to be involved with the

conversation that Fiona and Tim were going to be having with Michael. She could see that it was going to be difficult, and while she was a good friend of Fiona's, she felt that such marital matters were better left to the people most closely involved. Peter, her husband, was pottering in the garden. The garden was very formal with trees, bushes and lawns forming a geometric pattern that they found pleasing, but there was work to maintain it. Peter was trimming and snipping where necessary, more to enjoy the outdoor air, rather than any real need to do something particular. She walked out onto the pathway interspersing the box hedging,

'Fiona and Tim are going to talk to Michael this afternoon. Didn't think I would be welcome there,' she said. 'Could be a bit tricky.'

'I'm sure you're right,' Peter replied.

He continued his pottering. He was not keen on Paula getting too involved in Fiona's private life.

'Mind you,' Paula said, having second thoughts. 'Maybe I shouldn't have left her to it. Do you think that I should have gone and given her some moral support?'

'Paula,' said Peter. 'You know what I think. I have said it before. But it's up to you. She's your friend. What do you think she would want you to do?'

Paula walked back indoors, deep in thought. She had known Fiona for so many years, and when the idea had first been suggested at the pub last week, she had sensed that Fiona had been uncertain whether to confront Michael. She put the kettle on to make a cup of tea for Peter, and while she was waiting for it to boil, she decided to check her email. She logged on and there was a message from Danny. It was very cheery. It said all was well and he thought they would be coming home very soon. This was then followed by another message sent the following day, saying that they were due back in the UK on Sunday, and should be home on leave Monday. Paula was delighted, and called out into the back garden,

'Peter, Danny's coming home Monday.'

Peter looked up and smiled.

'Yes I know. I've seen it; I thought I would let you find out for yourself rather than telling you. Good news, isn't it?'

'Lovely, I must tell Fiona. I'll be back soon.'

'Not so quick,' said Peter. 'It'll keep for a bit. Where's that tea? Let's have a sit down on our own, and you can tell me all about this Tim chap.'

Paula agreed and poured the tea. As they sat quietly drinking it she told him the story up to date as she knew it, and he interrupted a couple of times with questions.

'You two have done a very thorough job, but what a can of worms you've opened. How are Fiona and Michael ever going to reconcile themselves with his background? I don't see how it could be done.'

'That is one reason why I think I ought to be there. I think Fiona is going to need some support when Michael gets to hear the whole story.'

'Why don't I come with you, then?' suggested Peter.

'OK then, come on,' agreed Paula.

Peter picked up the keys and they went out to the car.

'Better go round the back to park,' said Paula.

As they drove past the front of the shop they were surprised to see it in darkness. It was only just after half past four and they knew that Michael closed at half past five. Peter swung round behind the parade of shops into the small road that led to the flats. He stopped the car outside the kitchen window, and looking in he saw Michael and Tim squaring up to each other, and Michael had what looked like a carving knife in his hands. Peter went to get out of the car, but Paula stopped him.

'No! Don't do that! Call the police.'

Peter stopped and realised that Paula was right. He took out his mobile and dialled 999.

'Emergency. Which service do you require?'

'Police. There are two men fighting at Hopley Bookshop in the High Street. One of them has got a knife.'

The call continued with the operator requesting various details, but Peter was assured that there was help on the way. A few moments later he heard the reassuring sound of a police car siren, as it screeched into the High Street. At that moment the kitchen door opened and Fiona ran out, screaming. Peter got out of the car and she ran into his arms.

'He's got a knife! He'll kill him!'

By this time Paula was already out of the car and she took hold of Fiona.

'Get inside, come on,' she said, as she bundled Fiona into the back seat of the car and tried to comfort her.

Peter went across to the kitchen door just as police officers burst into the room. He could see Michael as he dropped the knife on to the floor, and another man, whom he took to be Tim, clutching at his stomach as blood spurted out. The police took Michael away, and he saw one of the other officers summoning an ambulance. The ambulance arrived shortly afterwards and the paramedics were able to staunch the blood flow and carry Tim out through the shop into the waiting vehicle at the front. A small crowd of late afternoon shoppers had gathered, watching as the well-respected bookshop owner was taken away in a police car, and an unknown man carried into the ambulance. Peter drove round to the front of the shop and Fiona was able to speak briefly with Tim before he lapsed into unconsciousness. She was anxious to follow him to the hospital in her own car, but Peter was adamant that that would be foolish and he offered to drive her there himself, which he did.

Michael Downing was looking somewhat dishevelled as he sat opposite Detective Inspector Brookes. Two hours in a Police cell following his arrest at the bookshop had given him space and time to think about what he was going to say. His solicitor had suggested to him that he should tell the whole story about Deborah, which had ultimately led to the confrontation with Tim. He was sure that Fiona, who had already spoken briefly to one of the officers at the shop as she was leaving for the hospital, and Tim, were he to survive, would certainly do so. He tried to get comfortable in the plastic chair and he began his tale.

He started with his marriage to Deborah, how it had all gone wrong, and how he had fallen in love with Louise. He continued with his story of the births of the children, and why he had given false information on the birth certificates. He explained what had happened when Deborah had walked out on him shortly after the birth, and how he and Louise had cheated to persuade the bank to transfer the funds out of Deborah's name, and into his. Telling the police the details of Grace's birth he did say that he was completely sure at the time that she was his child, and that he had not had any suspicion that Deborah might have had a lover.

'That's quite a list of admissions,' said Harry Brookes. 'But you haven't told us about the important one. Where is Deborah?'

'I told you,' said Michael. 'She walked out on me and I haven't heard of her since.'

'Then we can add bigamy to this list. When you married Louise you did not admit to having been married before, and you have no proof that Deborah is dead, do you?' said James Cook.

'No,' said Michael. 'But when Deborah walked out on me it seemed clear she was not going to be coming back. I had a small baby to look after. OK, I know that I had Louise as well, and it worked well for us to do what we did. But if Deborah hadn't gone, we would have had to work something else out. As it was, Louise and I decided to bring up the children as twins. It was easier that way.'

'I don't believe you,' said Brookes, looking him straight in the eye. 'This idea that a new mother would just walk out on her two day old baby is ludicrous. I think you murdered Deborah because she was in the way. It had always been your plan to dispose of Deborah somehow, and run off with Louise. What have you done with her body?'

'You're wrong,' replied Michael. 'You can charge me with all these other offences but I did not murder Deborah.'

'The sad end to the story...' he continued, '...was that one day when the twins were at nursery,

Louise decided to treat herself to a morning's clothes shopping at the new out-of-town shopping mall. I can see her now as she walked out to the car, as lovely as the day I first met her. Little did I realise it would be the last time I would see her alive. On her way home she was killed in a car crash. A German articulated lorry, whose driver was unaccustomed to driving on English roads, pulled out of a side road on to the wrong side of the road. Louise crashed into the lorry head-on. She was killed instantly; he escaped with just a bruised arm and chest.'

Michael sat back and took a drink of water from the glass in front of him.

'Now what about Tim Lock? Why did you stab him?' said Harry Brookes.

'It was a row. He and my wife Fiona found out about Deborah, and he claimed that he was Grace's father. He became aggressive and pushed me. I just grabbed what came to hand and lashed out with it. I was so angry. He had come to steal my child.'

'But she wasn't your child, was she?' said James Cook.

'No,' Michael agreed, sadly. 'But I didn't know that at the time.'

'Wounding is another one to add to the list, then,' said Brookes. 'James, take him away, we'll charge him later.'

James Cook escorted Michael back to the cells, and in the course of the next few days he was to be remanded in custody. Harry Brookes and his team were set on finding Deborah's body, as without it, a conviction on a murder charge would be very difficult.

Peter, Fiona and Paula had followed the ambulance to the local hospital on the edge of town. Fiona had two important telephone calls to make, but she wanted to make sure first of all that Tim was going to live. After an initial assessment the doctor told Fiona that the stab wound had not damaged any major organs, but that he must stay in hospital for the time being, and be given antibiotics to counteract any potential infection. They expected there to be no long-term damage. Leaving the hospital so she could use her mobile she rang Madeleine, whose number Tim had given her. She gave Tim's sister a brief description of what had happened and what the prognosis was, and Madeleine said she would come up to see Tim the following day.

The other call she had to make was going to be much more difficult. It was to the girls. She suggested that they came home so she could explain the full details, but she gave them a very brief outline on the phone. When they pointed out the lack of trains on a Sunday she said she would drive up to see them instead, and it was with trepidation that she made the journey on the following day. Fiona made up her mind during the drive there that she would be totally honest with them. There was, of course, quite different news for each girl.

On arrival she got straight to the point, explaining to them first of all that Tim was almost certainly Grace's father, and that her mother, Deborah, who had been Michael's first wife, had disappeared. Fiona said that as far as Victoria was concerned she was confident that Michael and Louise were her parents. She went on to tell them about the confrontation between Michael and Tim, Michael's arrest after the stabbing incident and Tim's hospitalisation. This news was shocking, but the uncertainties which had surrounded them since her previous visit had partially prepared them for something dreadful. Their remarkable resilience was shown when they insisted on coming home with Fiona to meet Tim.

Fiona brought the girls home from university. The bookshop would remain closed, and Fiona intended persuading Michael to put the business up for sale as soon as possible, as she did not feel able to continue with Michael's shadow hanging over it.

Grace and Victoria went with Fiona to visit Tim in hospital on the Tuesday. For Grace it was an odd experience, meeting her biological father for the first time in such strange circumstances, but when they were together Fiona noticed how alike they were. There was certainly no doubt any more as to who her father was. Naturally, Grace was finding it difficult to forgive the man she had always known as her father. She was still struggling with the full implications of what might have happened. That was going to take a long time to come to terms with. Tim told her of Michael's account of his relationship with Deborah, and how that contrasted with Deborah's version of events, as told by her to him. He also said how much he had loved Deborah, and how he was sure how much she, in her turn, had loved Grace, even if only for a very short time.

It was different for Victoria. When Fiona had told them the full story Victoria had found it very difficult to take in. The good, gentle man she had loved and respected as a father for all her life had been taken away from her, and replaced with a selfish, grasping, violent brute. She could not see any way in which she was going to be able to forgive him for that. Fortunately her sisterly relationship with Grace, who was now shown to be no relation at all, was strong enough to withstand these blows. She did retreat into her shell for a time, and some of her university work suffered as a result, but with Grace's and Andy's help she came through it.

Fiona was pleased to see that Tim was improving. Madeleine had been to see him on the Sunday, and he had been able to tell her, albeit briefly, what had happened with Michael. Fiona promised that she would contact Madeleine and tell her the full story; she thought she deserved that. Later in the week she took Tim a couple of books to read, and knowing his love of his garden, a large bunch of early spring flowers. They chatted for a while, not mentioning Michael and the 'incident', but talked just about

themselves, their likes and their dislikes, their families and their hopes for the future. When the nurse suggested to Fiona that it was time to leave she promised she would keep in touch, and perhaps travel down to Emberton to visit him when he was recovered.

Michael Downing had been returned to the cells, and James Cook and Harry Brookes were discussing their options over a coffee in Harry's office.

'Without a body it's going to be difficult,' said Harry. 'Have we spoken to Emberton police to see if there is anything that they can come up with?'

'Yes, they are having a look at their missing persons' file to start with. Initially they have not been able to find any report of a Deborah Downing going missing at all. If your wife had just given birth, and then walked out leaving you and the baby, wouldn't you contact the police? You'd be all over them. Well, nothing. He's done something with her. We just can't find out what,' said James.

'I have no doubt what he did, he killed her.

We just need to find the body, and then we'll prove it,'
said Harry confidently.

Further searches were instituted, questions were asked of local hospitals and further conversations held with all those involved, including Michael, but nothing came to light. Without a body Harry Brookes was not going to get his man. A date had been set for Michael's trial for the other offences, and he was still on remand.

Tim Lock had made a full recovery and was back at work in Emberton, looking forward to his new arrangement for part-time working, which was due to start in April. He was in regular contact with his daughter and Fiona, and even Victoria was being friendly towards him. It was as if he had acquired a completely new family, and he rather liked it. Madeleine had been fully informed of the new developments; she had met Grace on a couple of occasions, and was enjoying having a young woman in the family to talk to.

The bookshop was still up for sale, and there

had been one or two very positive enquiries which held out hope of progress. Fiona was continuing her work at Unity Insurance, but for the time being had given up on any more family history research. She was not sure that she wanted to uncover any more secrets. She began to spend more and more time with Tim, and would go and stay with him and Madeleine whenever she could. Madeleine would often find things to do away from home at these times, which Fiona found rather quaint, but she appreciated being able to spend time alone with Tim.

During one of these visits Tim was bringing Fiona up to date with his plans for an allotment, and what he intended growing there. He suggested that they have a walk through the town to have a look at where these were going to be. Walking along the High Street in Emberton they turned down a narrow lane past the Church, and then took a right turn into a road of solid red-brick houses,

'This is Edward Street,' he said. 'The allotments are going to be on a piece of waste ground at the far end. The council are clearing the site at the moment. There's so much rubbish there: shopping trolleys, rusty cars, old tyres, as well as scrubby trees and bushes. Nothing has been done with this bit of land for years, thirty or more I should think. It used to be an open market, but I believe that closed back in the sixties or seventies, when the supermarkets began to take over.'

They came to the end of the row of houses and the road petered out into a track and a field, with, as Tim had said, a load of junk. But as they got closer they could see a flashing blue light on the top of a police car, and blue and white tape cordoning off an area of ground. Further away was a white tent, into and out of which came men and women in white spacesuit-like outfits. One of the men took off his protective suit as they stood there, and they were surprised to recognise the smartly dressed figure of Inspector Henry Brookes, from Hopley.

They approached the cordon and Inspector Brookes called to them.

'No further! This is a police investigation.'

As he spoke he realised who the couple were and came over to them.

'It's Mr Lock and Mrs Downing isn't it?' he said. 'Harry Brookes, you may recognise me from Hopley. The council have unearthed some human remains whilst preparing the ground for some allotments. What are you doing here?'

Tim spoke;

'I live in Emberton and I've contracted to rent one of the allotments here when they are ready. Fiona is staying in Emberton and I brought her along to show her where they're going to be.'

'Do you know who lived in this street?' asked Harry.

'No, who?'

'Michael Downing's second wife, Louise.

Lived at number 22. Now we have found a body just up the road. Interesting.'

Tim went white.

'Do you think it is Deborah? Can you identify her?' he asked.

'We don't know if it is Deborah yet, but we will be able to find out. Dental records, DNA perhaps. That shouldn't be a problem. If it is, and I stress if, the next stage would be to prove that it was Michael or Louise who caused her death and put her here. We'll be in touch anyway. How long are you staying here, Mrs Downing, so that I know where to contact you if I need to?'

'You've got my mobile number, but I shall be here for a couple of days yet.'

Fiona and Tim moved away from the site. Tim was lost in thought, picturing how Michael might have brought Deborah here to bury her. It was a gruesome thought, but he could not help himself. He grimaced as he remembered her face, vibrant, happy and smiling that last time he saw her. He remembered how pleased she had been at the news of her pregnancy, and he knew that there was no chance that she would ever have left her baby, the baby she had been looking forward to so much. Tim and Fiona walked back through the town, in a very different mood from when they had set out on their afternoon stroll. As they walked she clasped his hand and he squeezed hers in return. They went inside the front door and she noticed there were tears in his eyes, and she kissed him gently and hugged him.

'Go and sit down and I will bring you a drink,' said Fiona.

He went into the living room and sat down on the settee. Fiona went into the kitchen and put the kettle. Then she came back and poured a large Scotch for Tim.

'Drink that, it'll make you feel better,' she said,

handing it to him.

'Thanks, you're a sweetheart.'

Fiona looked embarrassed; no one had called her that for a long time.

'We'll have to wait for a while before we know for certain whether that is Deborah, but I'm sure it is,' said Fiona.

'I'm sure you're right,' replied Tim. 'Come here, and he gently pulled Fiona towards him; she stumbled and she fell into his lap. He looked into her eyes and kissed her, and she kissed him back. They were still together when they heard Madeleine return. When she had come through and sat down they told her of their walk to Edward Street and what they had found there.

'The town's full of it,' said Madeleine. 'Every shop I went into was talking about it. Deborah Downing, that's who everybody says it is, not that anyone could know, and the town has decided that

Michael Downing is to blame.

It was early June and it had been two weeks since the body had been found at the allotment site. Harry Brookes was sitting in the office of Inspector Charles Burton of the Emberton police. As the body had been found at Emberton, and the crime probably committed there, it was Burton's case. With Downing already being under arrest for other offences in

Hopley, Brookes had been asked to assist. They had now confirmed the identity of the body as Deborah Downing by means of dental records, but were still searching for evidence that would link Michael Downing to the crime.

'He did it, Charlie,' said Harry. 'But we can't prove it. It's all circumstantial. His girlfriend lives nearby, his wife disappears, and the body turns up down the road. Bit too obvious, isn't it? No one else wanted her dead. I can't see another answer.'

'You're right,' agreed Burton. 'But just now we're stuck. When does Downing come up for trial on the other offences?'

'August, it's set for. I told him last time I spoke to him that we had identified the body, and that we were confident of finding the evidence to convict him. He was very gloomy, very unhelpful. Apparently he has been like this for some while now, according to the prison staff. It must be difficult at nearly sixty years old to go to prison, when you have had no connection with the criminal justice system before. It's an alien world.'

Just then the telephone on Burton's desk rang.

'Burton. Yes, he's here. Hunberton Remand Centre for you, Harry. Sounds as if we might have some interesting news.'

'Inspector Brookes speaking. Yes. What, today? I'll come straight away.'

'Michael Downing. He's topped himself. Do you want to come?' Harry said to his colleague.

'Yes,' replied Burton. 'I certainly do.'

It was just under an hour's drive to Hunberton Remand Centre, which was a modern facility, built in the 1990s to house men like Michael Downing, awaiting trial. It had been hoped when it was built that it would be 'softer' than prison, bearing in mind that the men there had not been convicted of any crime, but it had not worked out like that, and there was little obvious difference from a standard prison. Showing their warrant cards they entered the centre and were escorted to the governor's office. Here they were met by the governor, Mark Webber, a man in his late thirties, but whose appearance was that of someone approaching retirement. Harry Brookes thought that running a remand centre was clearly a job to age you even quicker than being a police officer.

Webber explained that Michael Downing had been low recently, but according to the doctor had not been clinically depressed. Downing had spoken of his concern at the possibility of receiving a long sentence as a result of his crimes, and had also been anxious about the Deborah Downing case, but had admitted nothing.

Webber explained that Downing's body had been found by one of his officers that morning, and they had summoned the doctor immediately, who confirmed that he was dead. The police and the Coroner's Office had been informed immediately. He had been able to hang himself by using bed sheets, an all too common method of suicide, so Webber said, but one which was difficult to guard against. He said there would be a post mortem, but there seemed little doubt as to the outcome. The governor then handed an unopened letter, which had been found near the body, to Harry, on the envelope of which was written '. As a matter of course Webber said that he would be contacting the next-of-kin, but he wondered whether Harry would also speak to Mrs Downing, as he had met her. Harry agreed that he would.

He put the letter into his jacket pocket. It was no business of the remand centre governor's, and he wanted to be able to read what he expected would be a confession in the comfort of his own, or, at least, Charlie Burton's, office. The two policemen drove back to Emberton, both thankful that this case seemed to be coming to a satisfactory conclusion. They both realised that without a confession it was unlikely that Deborah Downing's murderer would have ever been brought to book. On arriving back at Burton's office Harry copied the letter and gave one copy to Charlie Burton.

'Now we can read it together, but separately,' he said.

They started to read:

After your last visit when you told me that you had identified Deborah's body I started thinking. I know that I am likely to receive a substantial prison sentence for what I have done. Prison has been difficult for me, and the thought of more years behind bars is too much to contemplate. That is why I will be dead by the time you read this letter. Having made this decision I wanted to clear my conscience about Deborah as well. The story I told you after I was arrested was true up until the time that Grace was born, and this is the truth of what happened after that. However, I do want to explain the reasons as well as the actions. Louise was my passion and I would have done anything she wanted me to do. Throughout her life she had always been a person who got what she wanted, and she wanted me as much as I wanted her.

When I told her of Deborah's pregnancy, she feared that I might stay with my wife, and desert her and her unborn child. However this was not to be as I was as determined as she was for us to be together. I was fed up with Deborah and her behaviour towards me, her constant complaints and scrutiny of my every move. Between us, Louise and I formulated a plan that, after the birth, and after the initial post-natal visits, Deborah would disappear. We would move to a new area, with the two children, apparently as man and wife. Louise had already sold her house before Victoria was born, and was living in rented accommodation by the time she arrived.

The plan worked near-perfectly. When Grace was born, I was entranced by her, believing, *incorrectly as it turned out, that she was my child. I could have just left Deborah and gone to live with Louise, but that way I would have lost the bookshop, bought with the proceeds of the sale of Deborah's mother's house, lost my daughter Grace and lost access to the remains of Deborah's savings. The move to the bookshop was scheduled for 14th March 1993, a few days after Grace's birth. I admit I registered both girls as mine and Louise's, but on different days. I did this because I had already registered Victoria's birth before Grace had been born. Then, on Grace's birth, I realised I should have waited and registered them together as twins. To get over this I registered Grace with the same details as Victoria, making it look as though they were twins. Eventually it was this error that led to my downfall.*

I realise that my selfish desires have brought

me to this situation. I had wanted Deborah's money,

her house, and her baby, but not Deborah. I wanted

Louise and her baby. But now I have nothing.

Deborah and Louise are both dead, the baby was not

mine but Tim Lock's, the money is all spent, and my

business is probably in ruins. My only daughter,

Victoria, will surely disown me, and I have betrayed

my wife Fiona, who has done nothing to deserve what

I have brought upon her.

Apologies are futile, but tell Fiona and the

girls that I really did love them.

Michael Downing

'That seems fairly conclusive,' said Harry. 'I

think it provides the answers to all our questions. I'll

get on to Fiona Downing tomorrow and fill her in with

all the details. I don't think there will be anything else

on this case.'

He stood up and shook hands with Charlie Burton.

'Thanks for your help. Nice and easy in the end.'

Harry Brookes had already spoken to Fiona on the phone before he went to see her the following morning. She was still living over the bookshop, pending the sale of the flat and the business. She read the letter carefully and without emotion. During the weeks since this had blown up she had become immune to any further shocking revelations. She could see from the letter that Michael's relationship with Louise was clearly the driving force behind everything that he had done, and she, Louise, had a lot to answer for. The remand centre authorities had asked her to make the appropriate funeral arrangements, as Michael was not a convicted prisoner. This she undertook to do. It was, by now, the summer term and Grace and Victoria were back at university. Fiona had spoken to them and told them what had happened and what the letter said, and said she would send them a copy so they could see it for themselves. They had been expecting bad news of one sort or another, but this was about the worst news there could possibly have been. Fiona was amazed at the fortitude shown by the girls and how their love and care for one another helped them deal with these exceptional circumstances.

On reading Michael's letter Fiona understood all those little puzzles which had come to light during her family history quest, and she was pleased that Harry had provided her with a copy. She thanked him for all he had done to help her over the weeks. She was pleased that Deborah could now have a proper burial and the girls could concentrate on their university careers. The bookshop sale was progressing satisfactorily and she hoped that it would all be finished by the beginning of July, when she was planning to start a new phase in her life. She rang Paula and said she would email a copy of the letter so she could see the full story.

Afterword

Tim and Fiona were married later that year and shortly afterwards Fiona was delighted to discover that she was pregnant. On telling Tim excitedly, she stopped short, a thought suddenly crossing her mind ; all those years with Michael and no babies....maybe Victoria wasn't his either.

Printed in Great Britain
by Amazon

87570760R00220